P9-CRQ-426

The Bobbsey twins welcomed the ferryboat's
first passengers

THE
BOBBSEY TWINS'
OWN LITTLE
FERRYBOAT

By LAURA LEE HOPE

Publishers
GROSSET & DUNLAP
NEW YORK

© GROSSET & DUNLAP 1956
ALL RIGHTS RESERVED
ISBN: 0-448-08049-4

PRINTED IN THE UNITED STATES OF AMERICA

The Bobbsey Twins' Own Little Ferryboat

CONTENTS

CHAPTER I

AN EXCITING PROMISE

"LET'S have our fortunes told, Freddie!" said blond, curly-haired Flossie Bobbsey.

"That will be fun," her brother agreed. "The fortuneteller is Tara, the gypsy girl in Nan's class."

The big blue eyes of the six-year-old twins blinked with delight as they gazed about the fair being held in their school gymnasium.

The room was filled with children and grown-ups milling about from booth to booth. Above the babble of voices came a lively tune over a loudspeaker. The air was full of excitement and the wonderful aroma of buttered popcorn, chocolate cake, and cinnamon candy.

"Do you think we should go to the fortune-teller's alone?" Flossie hunched her shoulders and giggled.

"It does look dark and spooky in Tara's tent," Freddie said. "Let's ask Nan to take us."

Nan, the little twins' dark-haired, brown-eyed sister, was twelve. She also had a twin, Bert, a slender, happy boy who looked much like her.

Right now Nan and Bert were very busy. Bert was in charge of a fish-pond game, while Nan and her friend Nellie Parks were selling cakes and candies at a near-by table.

"There's Nan," Freddie said. He and Flossie skipped across the floor toward her.

Hearing their merry voices as they approached, Nan looked up and called, "Hi! Having a good time?"

"We sure are!" Freddie exclaimed. He jingled a pocketful of nickels and dimes. "Flossie and I played ring-toss, and dropped pennies into a milk bottle—"

"And threw darts at big balloons!" concluded Flossie. "Now we want to have our fortunes told," she added, jumping up and down.

"Maybe you'd like some candy first," Nellie Parks suggested, winking at Nan. She was a pretty girl with dark blond hair and blue eyes. Nellie and Nan had thought up the idea of running the cake-and-candy booth together.

As Flossie and Freddie chorused, "Oh yes," Nellie scooped up two chunks of fudge from the bottom of a square pan.

"I'll treat you," Nellie said, and dropped two nickels into the money box on her table. Thanking her, Flossie and Freddie started to nibble the fudge.

Nan sighed as she looked first at the money box, then around the gym. "I hope we make a lot of money at this fair."

"So do I," Nellie said earnestly.

She and the older Bobbseys were pupils in the class which had organized the event.

The purpose of the fair was to raise money for new stage equipment and properties for the school Dramatic Club. Although the school board had offered to help, a good deal of extra money was still needed.

Freddie and Flossie were becoming impatient. The little girl tugged at Nan's hand. "Please take us to the fortuneteller's," she begged. "Let's go now!"

"Go ahead, Nan," Nellie urged. "I'll manage all right alone till you come back."

As Nan stepped from behind the counter, a boy walked up and eyed the cake and candy.

"Hello, Danny," Nan greeted him. "Would you like to buy something?"

Danny Rugg, as tall as Bert but heavier, usually scowled more than he smiled. He was known for his mean tricks and seemed to delight in annoying the Bobbseys.

"Maybe I'll buy something and maybe I won't!" Danny announced.

"Here's something nice for seventy-five cents," Nellie said helpfully, lifting a two-layered chocolate cake off the table for Danny's inspection.

"Hmmmmm," he muttered. "Not bad looking, but how does it taste?"

"Extra-special!" Freddie said with enthusiasm. "Because Nan baked it."

"Oh, yes?" Danny sneered. "In that case I'd better sample it." Before Nellie Parks could stop him, Danny took the cake from her.

Holding it in his left hand, Danny swiftly ran a finger across the top, scooping up some of the chocolate. Then he popped his finger into his mouth.

Nan was aghast as she looked at the streaked icing. "You horrid boy!" she cried out.

"Ugh! This tastes awful!" Danny said, making a face. "You can have it back!"

Nan, Flossie, and Nellie eyed him angrily as Freddie cried, "You have to pay for it!" and tugged at Danny's arm.

"Hey, get away!" Danny shouted, and gave Freddie a shove. The small boy teetered backward and Danny, too, lost his balance on the slippery gymnasium floor.

As the older boy skidded to one knee, the cake

which he held flew into the air and with a loud *plop* landed on Freddie's head! The cake broke into a dozen pieces and fell to the floor.

"Danny!" screamed Flossie, beating at him with her chubby fists. "Look what you've done to my brother!" Tears of anger began to run down her pink cheeks.

Before anyone could stop Danny, he sprang to his feet and ran off through the crowd. Now several persons gathered around Freddie, who was trying, with Nan's help, to brush the sticky chocolate from his head.

"What happened?" shouted Bert as he ran over to help.

When Nan told him how Danny had spoiled her chocolate cake and made it fall on Freddie, Bert vowed to get even with the bully, but added, "I can't leave the pond for long."

"Please help Freddie wash the chocolate off his hair," Nan asked her twin.

"Come on, Freddie. We'll get you cleaned off," Bert said as he took the little boy by the hand and led him to the locker room.

While they were gone, the girls got a pail of water and some cloths and removed the remains of the cake from the floor.

In a few minutes, Freddie returned with his face and hair clean, but with some spots of chocolate left on his white shirt.

"Well, we were going to have our fortunes told, weren't we?" Nan said gaily, trying to make the younger twins forget the mishap. "Let's go see Tara now."

They headed for the small tent which had a draped entrance to keep people from looking inside. In front of it sat a lovely, black-haired girl about Nan's age but not as tall. She wore a white, short-sleeved blouse and a full skirt which hung in folds of vivid red, yellow, and green.

A white lace mantilla covered her head and hung loosely over both shoulders. In the center of it was a large gold coin engraved in a leaf design.

"Hello, Nan," the girl said, smiling.

Nan knew that her classmate, who had beautiful dark eyes, long lashes, and an olive complexion, was only half gypsy. While her mother had come from a gypsy clan in Spain, Tara's father was an Irish-American named O'Toole. Tara had the good looks and charm of both nationalities.

"How pretty you look, Tara," said Nan. "I've brought some more customers. This is my little sister Flossie and my brother Freddie," she continued. "They want to have their fortunes told."

"Good, but first you all must cross my palm with silver!" Tara giggled. "Then you may come inside my tent one at a time."

Freddie, Flossie, and Nan took dimes from their pockets and laid them in Tara's left hand.

"Thank you," she said. "You come in first, Nan." She pulled aside the flap of the tent and the two girls went in.

"I wonder what's going on," Freddie whispered to his sister as they heard Tara begin to talk.

"Let's peek," Flossie suggested.

They parted the drapes just a little and looked inside. Nan was seated on a bench across from Tara, who was examining her right hand.

"Nan, the lines on your palm tell me you're a sweet, sincere, and helpful girl liked by everyone. You will have a happy life."

Tara studied Nan's hand again and said, "I see a letter—and there's a gift and great excitement in store for you!"

Nan smiled when she heard this. She and the other Bobbseys loved surprises. She asked Tara to tell her more about the letter and the gift.

Tara shook her head wisely and said, "Wait and see!"

Still curious, but realizing that Tara was not going to explain further, Nan thanked her. "Now will you tell Flossie's and Freddie's fortunes?" she asked.

"Here we are already," said the little boy, as he and his twin popped inside the tent.

"I see a gift coming to you, Nan,"
said the young fortuneteller

"Can you tell our fortunes together?" Flossie asked eagerly.

"All right," said Tara, and they sat down side by side on the bench. "Since you're twins and play with each other a lot, many of the same things will happen to both of you."

Flossie and Freddie smiled and extended their right hands on the table top. Their hearts were pounding with excitement. What would they learn?

"The lines in your hands are not the same," Tara said. "Freddie, it seems, gets into more trouble than his twin."

Flossie giggled, as her brother bobbed his head in agreement.

Tara turned to Flossie's hand. "I see, though, that you always try to help your twin."

"What else can you see?" Flossie asked, her eyelashes fluttering like a butterfly's wings. "Is there something good?"

"Yes," Tara said in a hushed whisper as Nan looked on.

"Tell us! Please tell us!" Flossie urged.

"You will have a wonderful surprise very soon," Tara announced, her dark eyes flashing.

"When is soon?" Freddie asked.

"This summer," Tara continued, smiling, "both of you will spend a lot of time crossing water!"

CHAPTER II

SUSPICIOUS STRANGERS

THE promise of crossing water thrilled Freddie and Flossie.

"It'll be a bee-yoo-ti-ful summer!" the small girl cried excitedly. "Will we take a boat trip 'cross the ocean, Tara?"

"Or a canoe ride down a river?" Freddie interrupted. There was a river near by that emptied into Lake Metoka, on which the Bobbseys' town of Lakeport was situated.

Nan laughed. "Tell them what kind of water they'll cross," she urged Tara, "or Flossie and Freddie will never get to sleep tonight."

The young fortuneteller smiled and studied the children's palms again. "I can see no more," she said. "I can read what will happen to you, but not how it will come about. But don't pack your suitcases yet," she joked. "Like Nan, you must wait."

Freddie stood up, looking disappointed. "Okay," he sighed. Then his chubby face brightened. "Would you show us how to tell fortunes, Tara, 'cause I'd like to read our pets' paws!"

Nan and Tara burst into laughter, but Flossie said seriously, "I'd like to know, too. We have three pets, two dogs named Snap and Waggo, and a cat, Snoop."

Tara said she did not think that palm-reading would work on animals—at least not the kind that was used for human beings.

"Besides," she added, as another customer stopped at the tent, "fortunetelling takes years of study. I've only learned a little. But if you'll come to my house some time, I'll tell you what I know."

The Bobbseys accepted the invitation, then thanked Tara and left the tent.

What thoughts of adventure danced through their heads! Their last one had been *On A Bicycle Trip*. During the trip the twins had uncovered a mystery about several lost articles.

"I can hardly wait to know about crossing water," said Freddie.

In the meantime, there were exciting things for the children to do at the fair.

"I'm going to help Nan sell candy," Flossie said, as she skipped off with her sister.

"And I'm going to catch a prize in Bert's fish

pond," Freddie announced. He wandered over to where his brother was helping a group of youngsters with their poles.

The "pond" was a large, plastic wading pool which the Bobbseys had been given the summer before. It held so much water that Flossie and Freddie could actually swim in it.

As Freddie walked up, Bert was handing a pole to Teddy Blake, a six-year-old friend of Freddie's.

"This is how it works," Bert explained to Teddy. "There's a magnet on the end of the string, instead of a hook." He added that the fish pond was full of little metal trinkets.

"The first one your magnet picks up is your prize," said Bert. "You get only one try."

Teddy quickly dangled his line deep into the water. A second later he exclaimed, "Hurray, I've got something!" Pulling out a tin whistle, he cried happily, "Oh boy! This is just what I need for calling my dog."

"May I have a turn, please?" Freddie asked Bert. "Hope I get something as good!"

"Sure, but it'll cost you a dime," Bert grinned.

Freddie handed him the money and selected a pole. Then he dangled his line in the fish pond. When he pulled it out Freddie gave a whoop of joy, for stuck to his "hook" was a tiny, bright red fire engine!

"Look—a baby one just like my big toy fire engine!" he exclaimed.

Freddie loved fire engines, real ones and toy ones. In fact, that was why Mr. Bobbsey had nicknamed his small son his "Little Fat Fireman." Freddie's favorite plaything was a fire engine with a rubber hose that squirted water from a small tank. It had been given to him as a birthday present.

"Bert, your fish pond is keen!" he said. "I'll carry my prize in my pocket all the time."

Just then a little girl approached, handed Bert a dollar bill, and asked for a chance to fish. "I hope I catch a doll," she said.

"I can't change your dollar," said Bert, as he gave her a line. He turned to Freddie. "Will you mind the pond while I get some nickels and dimes from Nan?"

Freddie said he would, feeling very proud to take over this duty. As Bert walked off, several of Freddie's schoolmates came over to play the game. Freddie took their dimes and handed out fishing lines.

Suddenly he noticed that Danny Rugg was edging toward the side of the plastic pool, pushing the smaller boys out of the way.

"You get out of here!" Freddie cried, as the bully came closer. He looked frantically around for Bert, who was nowhere in sight.

"You got me into a lot of trouble," Danny said in a low voice as he sidled up to Freddie.

"What do you mean?" Freddie exclaimed. "You ruined the cake, but I was the one it fell on!"

Danny scowled. "My mother heard about the cake and made me pay Nan seventy-five cents out of my allowance. It's all your fault!"

"You leave Freddie alone!" challenged Teddy Blake, "or you'll be sorry."

The bully, of course, knew that Freddie Bobbsey was not to blame for the cake incident. Nevertheless, he had to take out his ill temper on someone.

"For two cents I'd push you right in the water," he hissed. "By cracky, I think I'll do it!"

Danny lunged forward to grab Freddie Bobbsey, but this time the small boy was ready for him. Ducking quickly to one side, Freddie thrust out his foot. The bully tripped and lost his balance.

SPLASH! He landed square in the fish pond. Water flew up from the pool, spraying the children near by. Danny Rugg stood up, wringing wet. Boys and girls began to snicker.

"Oh, you think it's funny!" Danny stormed angrily. "Well, you try it. I never want to see this old fish pond—"

As he started to step out of the pool, he slipped

and went back into the water! The children howled with laughter. The bully was getting just what he deserved!

Danny shamefacedly crawled from the pool and quickly made his exit from the gymnasium, leaving a trail of wet footprints behind him.

Instantly Freddie became a hero among his small friends, who now gathered to spend their money at the fish pond. By the time Bert returned with the change, his small brother had a big handful of dimes to give him.

Flossie, meanwhile, had tired of helping her sister at the candy booth. Still intrigued by the fortunetelling, she wandered back to Tara's booth. Since the curtains were drawn Flossie assumed Tara had a customer.

When several minutes went by and the young fortuneteller did not appear, Flossie began to fidget. "Tara must be telling someone an awful, awful long fortune," she thought, and edged closer to the entrance of the black tent.

As Flossie waited, she heard voices inside. It sounded as if two grownups, a man and a woman, were talking to Tara. Suddenly the voices became louder.

"Could they be arguing?" Flossie thought. "And what could they be arguing about? Tara tells such nice fortunes."

Now the two grownups' voices sounded angry. Flossie could no longer hold back her curiosity. Tiptoeing quietly to the curtain, she pulled it aside just enough to peek through with one eye.

Inside, Tara was seated at the table, with a man and a woman directly across from her. The woman had light, almost white, fuzzy hair and wore a polka-dot dress. The man, also blond, had a small, bristly mustache.

"We must have it," the woman said, pointing to the lovely white headdress which Tara was wearing.

"But I won't sell it," Tara protested. "It's very old, and—"

"Where did you get it?" the woman demanded.

"From my grandmother. She's a real gypsy and lives in Spain," Tara answered.

"We don't care about that," the man said tartly. "We admire your mantilla and would like to buy it. Come on! Don't be foolish. You can get another."

"But I can't," Tara said tearfully, looking around as if hoping someone would come to her aid.

Flossie's heart raced with excitement as the man shouted, "Here, I'll give you ten dollars for that mantilla!"

He pulled out his wallet, and instantly Flossie noticed how fat it was. And when he opened the billfold, the little girl's eyes popped, for it was stuffed with money.

"There, will that be enough?" the stranger said as he whipped out a crisp ten-dollar bill and held it toward Tara.

When the girl started to weep softly, the woman became furious. "All right, give her twenty!" she hissed. "I must have that mantilla!"

At that moment, Tara glanced toward the flap of the tent. She caught a glimpse of Flossie, and as if giving her a signal, burst out in tears.

Tara seemed so frightened that Flossie decided to call for help. She glanced around the gymnasium. Off to one side the little girl spotted the school principal, a nice-looking, slender man in a gray suit. His hair was thin and he wore glasses.

"Mr. Tetlow! Mr. Tetlow!" Flossie cried, running up to him.

"What is it, Flossie? Don't you feel well?"

"It's not that," the little girl said, tugging at his hand. "Come quick before they hurt her."

"Hurt whom?" the principal asked, perplexed.

"Tara! She needs help!"

CHAPTER III

THE MISSING PET

FLOSSIE'S pleas alarmed Mr. Tetlow. He put his arm around her shoulders. "What's the matter? Why does Tara need help?" he asked.

Flossie quickly explained the situation as she led the kindly man toward Tara's tent. The couple had left and were halfway to a door.

"Stop! Wait!" Mr. Tetlow cried, but the man and woman paid no heed.

Before the principal could catch them, they had made their way through the crowded room and hurried out an exit. Though Flossie and Mr. Tetlow looked for them, the couple had vanished.

"Oh, I hope that Tara is all right," the little girl said as she and the principal came back and parted the curtains of the fortuneteller's tent. Tara was sitting at the table, her head resting on her hands, and she was sobbing pitifully.

"Did those bad people hurt you?" Flossie asked, hurrying to the gypsy girl's side.

Tara said no. Then, drying her eyes, she told Mr. Tetlow that the man and woman had threatened her, saying she would be sorry for not selling the mantilla.

"I thought they were going to snatch it away from me," Tara said. "But they heard Flossie calling you, Mr. Tetlow, and ran away."

Tara added that she had never seen the couple before and wondered if Mr. Tetlow had.

"No," he replied, "but perhaps some of the other folks here know them."

The principal stepped outside the tent, where a crowd had gathered after hearing Flossie's cries. Bert and Nan were among them. Mr. Tetlow asked if any of them knew the couple, but all the listeners shook their heads.

"They must be strangers in town," Bert remarked. "We'll be on the lookout for them, Mr. Tetlow."

As the Bobbsey children comforted Tara, Mr. Tetlow confided to them that he had some more bad news. "Even though our school fair is a good one," he said, "I don't believe we'll make enough money to reach our goal."

"Oh dear," Nan said. "Then we won't be able to have that wonderful school play we planned for next fall"

"Sure we can," Bert said.

"How?"

"We can raise the money during the summer-time."

When Nan asked what her brother had in mind, Bert said he did not have any ideas at the moment, but he thought that after the school term was over, they could surely find a way to raise the needed money.

"That'll be fine, if it can be worked out," Mr. Tetlow said. "I hope you succeed, Bert. Good luck!"

The fair finally came to an end late in the afternoon and the four Bobbsey twins headed toward home.

"Let's keep looking for those strangers who scared Tara," Nan said, as they walked down a pleasant, tree-lined street.

"Yes," Bert agreed. "I wonder why Tara's headdress was so important to them?" The other twins were also puzzled.

Although they looked up one street and down another, they saw no sign of the mysterious strangers. Finally they reached home.

As the twins crossed the front lawn of their spacious home, they saw a man on his hands and knees peering beneath the shrubbery at the side of the house.

"It's Sam," Freddie announced. "I wonder if

he's hunting for the same people we are!"

Sam Johnson was a jolly Negro who had worked at Mr. Bobbsey's lumberyard for years. His wife Dinah helped the twins' mother with the housework. The couple lived on the third floor of the Bobbsey home, and Sam sometimes acted as handyman around the house.

"Hi there, Sam!" Bert called out. "Did you lose something?"

The gray-haired man stood up, took a red checkered handkerchief from his pocket, and mopped his brow. "Sure did," he said, "and Dinah is plenty worried."

Just then Dinah herself appeared around the corner of the house, a flowered apron tied around her large waist.

"Hello, honey lambs," she said. "I'm so glad you're home to help hunt. After he ate his biscuits he just disappeared. Something must have happened to him!"

"Biscuits? What's this all about, Dinah?" Nan asked puzzled.

The cook turned her big brown eyes toward her husband. "Didn't you tell the twins that Waggo was gone?" she asked.

"I didn't have time," came Sam's reply.

"Well, you're just slow as taffy pulling, Sam Johnson," Dinah exclaimed, standing with her hands on her hips. Then she added, "That dog

Waggo disappeared three hours ago and I'm just worried sick about him."

Waggo was a peppy fox terrier whom the Bobbseys had had for some time. When Waggo was happy his tail wagged back and forth so fast that it was just a white blur. That was how he got his name. Waggo played with Snap, the older dog, and also loved to tease Snoop, the black cat, with his playfulness.

"We'll find Waggo," Freddie said, acting very important. "Here, Waggo, here, Waggo!" he called loudly.

"He's nowhere near here," Sam said. "I've been calling that dog for half an hour."

"We'll all look for him," Bert said, wondering where the pet might have gone.

"But don't be late for dinner," Dinah warned, " 'cause we're having roast beef, with lemon meringue pie for dessert."

"Yummy!" said Flossie, as all four twins hurried off to look for Waggo.

Halfway down the street they met Susie Larker, a chestnut-haired friend of Flossie's.

"Where are you going?" Susie asked, because it was unusual to see both sets of twins walking in the same direction at the same time.

"Waggo's lost," Flossie said sadly.

"Oh, I saw him," Susie said breezily. "He was chasing a big boxer down that way!" She pointed down the road which led toward a patch of woods a quarter of a mile away.

After thanking Susie, the Bobbseys hurried in this direction. Their pet sometimes liked to romp in the woods, but before this he had never been gone for so long.

"Do you suppose something's happened to Waggo?" Flossie asked fearfully.

"Maybe a bear scared him," Freddie shuddered, even though he knew there were no bears in Lakeport.

"Oh, I think Waggo's safe," Nan said, trying to calm her sister's fears. "Probably he met a dog friend and just forgot to come home."

But the young twins were not convinced as they made their way into the woods. Suddenly Freddie stopped. "Ssh! What's that?"

The other children listened. Somewhere in the distance came the sound of a dog whining!

"That's Waggo all right!" Bert exclaimed. "Come! Hurry!"

He led the way with his brother and sisters following. The sound of Waggo's whining grew louder and more pitiful as they came to a little stream, on the other side of which was a broken-down split-rail fence.

Skipping across the little stream on three flat stones, the children ran up to the fence where the whining was louder. The split rails had once served as a boundary line between two farms and were strung with rusty barbed wire to keep animals from passing through.

"Waggo, Waggo!" Flossie cried out. "Where are you?"

"*Yip, yip,*" came the dog's pitiful reply.

"Oh, there he is! I see him!" Nan shouted.

Waggo was lying on the ground several yards away. His collar had become entangled in a piece of the barbed wire and he could not get free.

Bert rushed up to the dog and told him to hold still. Then he carefully twisted the jagged wire from the dog's collar.

"Is he hurt?" Flossie asked nervously, as she saw some pieces of Waggo's fur clinging to the rusty barbs.

Nan examined the terrier. "I don't think so," she said. "Waggo's just frightened."

"Arf! Arf!" Waggo barked, happy to be released. He skipped from one twin to another and ran around them in circles.

"We'd better take this piece of barbed wire home and throw it in the trash can," Nan said. "Then no other animal can get hurt by it."

Bert pulled up the rusty piece and held it out as they walked back home. How relieved Dinah was to see Waggo again! As the dog bounded into the kitchen, she knelt down and scooped the terrier up lovingly.

"Oh, Waggo, I'm so glad you're all right," she cried. Then Dinah hurried into the pantry and reached into the cooky jar. "To show you how happy I am," she said, "you can have a cooky."

As Waggo gulped the cooky, Freddie said wistfully, "May we have one too, Dinah?" The small boy loved to eat and was always being teased about his appetite.

Dinah chuckled. "Just a little one," she said. "Dinner is nearly ready."

All the twins munched cookies as they walked into the living room. There Mr. Bobbsey, a tall, good-looking man, was reading a letter to his attractive wife. The youthful-looking parents were full of fun and enjoyed having good times with their twins.

At once Flossie told the news about the mysterious strangers at the fair, and Freddie went into a detailed report of finding Waggo.

Mr. Bobbsey smiled. "Now," he said, "I have some news of my own for you children."

"What is it, Daddy?" Freddie asked.

"A surprise, my Fat Fireman," he said.

Mrs. Bobbsey smiled as her husband said, "Remember my telling you about an old farmer named Homer Wiggins?"

Nan nodded. "You mean the man whose barn you helped rebuild after it burned down?"

"That's right," said Mr. Bobbsey. "Well, now he wants to do a favor for me in return."

Mrs. Bobbsey spoke up. "Read the letter aloud, Dick."

The children's father read the message which he had received that afternoon. Mr. Wiggins asked that the family call on him at his farm on the shore of Lake Metoka very soon.

"And the surprise," Mr. Bobbsey went on, "is a gift for you twins."

"A gift for us!" the four children shouted. "What is it?"

"Mr. Wiggins doesn't say. But I'm sure it's a fine one."

Instantly Nan recalled what Tara had told when reading her fortune. She would receive a letter and a gift and have great excitement. Part of it was already coming true!

CHAPTER IV

FRISKY CALVES

EXCITED and curious about Mr. Wiggins' surprise, the Bobbsey twins hardly heard Dinah announce that dinner was ready.

"Tell us more about the farmer, Dad," Bert requested as he held the dining-room chair for his mother to be seated.

While the family ate Dinah's juicy roast beef, Mr. Bobbsey explained that Mr. Wiggins was planning to move away from Lakeport in two months. The surprise he had mentioned concerned this.

"What can it be?" Nan wondered.

"I cannot imagine," her mother replied.

Finally the talk shifted to the school fair. Mr. and Mrs. Bobbsey were sorry to learn that enough money had not been raised. They thought, however, that Bert's idea for a summer project was a good one.

"Let's have a grape juice stand," Flossie suggested. "Last summer we earned forty-six cents that way!"

"But we need to earn a LOT of money," Nan told her. "Forty-six cents would not be nearly enough."

Freddie thought that he might run errands for the groceryman. It was finally decided that it would be more fun to plan a project that all four children could run.

"But what?" puzzled Flossie.

Mrs. Bobbsey smiled and said, "I'm sure you'll find something worthwhile to do. Your father and I will try to help you think of a scheme."

"We could all be fortunetellers," Flossie said earnestly, "and Nan could make turbans for us to wear." Everyone chuckled and the conversation switched to Tara.

"I know Tara's a talented girl," Mrs. Bobbsey said, as the family began eating lemon meringue pie. "But that's not strange because both her parents are talented too."

As Freddie wiped a bit of meringue from the tip of his nose, Mrs. Bobbsey said that recently there had been an article in the newspaper about Tara's father.

"Mr. O'Toole is a famous painter," she said. "He is now making a tour of the Caribbean

Islands, where he will paint a series of pictures of the native people there."

"Are we natives?" Flossie piped up.

"Yes, we are, my Little Fat Fairy," her father answered. "We're natives of Lakeport."

"But we don't wear grass skirts or carry spears," Flossie said, looking puzzled.

"And we're not like the Eskimos," Freddie said, agreeing with his sister. "We don't eat blubber and ride in kayaks."

The other Bobbseys laughed and Nan explained, "You don't have to be born in a part of the world where clothes and food are different from ours. That only means if you were born in a certain place, such as Lakeport, you're a native of it."

Although this was not entirely clear to Freddie, he nodded his head importantly as if he understood it all very well.

Mrs. Bobbsey spoke up. "You see, Tara's gypsy mother is a native of Spain. That means she was born in that country."

At the mention of the word, "gypsy," all the twins listened with rapt attention as Mrs. Bobbsey went on. "Tara's mother is a beautiful woman. Not only can she sing well, but she is a fine actress and dancer. This year she will appear in the Lakeport summer-stock theater. Tourists from all over will come here to see her perform."

"Won't it be fun to visit Tara's home," Nan said as the family arose from the table. "Maybe her mother will dance and sing for us."

"But I want to learn about our surprise first," Freddie chimed in. "Can't we go to Mr. Wiggins' farm tomorrow?"

"That's right, Dad," Bert said. "It's Saturday and there's no school. Besides, you close the lumberyard at noon so you'd be free to take us."

"It's a deal," Mr. Bobbsey announced, smiling. "We'll visit Mr. Wiggins tomorrow."

The children were so excited about the next day's fun that they could hardly wait for morning to come. Both sets of twins were up early, for each of them had certain chores to do on Saturday mornings. Bert always cut the grass while Nan weeded the garden.

Meanwhile, the small twins went to the store for their mother, who had forgotten a couple of articles while shopping the day before.

"Golly, I hope it gets to be twelve o'clock soon," Freddie said, as he and Flossie returned from the store with a can of cinnamon and a box of raisins.

"So do I," said Flossie, walking into the Bobbseys' kitchen where Dinah was busy kneading dough for sugar buns. "Oh, that looks like fun," she said, watching Dinah's competent hands twist, turn, roll, and pat the dough. Dinah liked to do her baking from start to finish, as she put it, not buying her bread "half baked" in a store.

"Let me try that," Freddie begged and Flossie said, "Me too!"

Dinah chuckled. "All right, sweetie-pies. But put on aprons."

"I'd look funny in an apron," Freddie protested. "They're for ladies!"

"That's not so," Dinah stated. "Famous men chefs always wear them."

"They have high white hats to go with the aprons," said Freddie.

"I'll soon fix that," Dinah laughed. She washed her hands and went for a roll of white shelf paper.

In a few minutes she had made two hats that looked like giant mushrooms, and set them on the twins' heads. Flossie had already found white aprons, and these were tied around the children.

Dinah cut off pieces from the platter of dough and handed them to the children. They pulled and pushed at the white lumps. Within five minutes their fingers were covered with sticky paste and they could not get it off!

"What'll I do, Dinah?" Flossie said, worried.

Laughing, Dinah came to the rescue. She sprinkled flour on the twins' hands and helped to peel the dough off. After that the kneading went smoothly, and soon the cinnamon and raisins were added, and the pan of sugar buns was set on a shelf to rise.

Flossie and Freddie peeked at them every few minutes during the next hour as the dough rose higher and higher. Finally Dinah said the buns were ready for the oven.

When they were baked and Dinah was ready, Freddie took out three from one end of the pan. "These are the ones I made," he said proudly. "I'm going to be a chef when I grow up."

Flossie and Dinah laughed. Freddie changed his mind every day about what he wanted to be. Already he had decided on fireman, policeman, detective, and candy-store owner!

"Here comes Daddy!" Flossie announced, as her father drove in with Sam. "Now we can go see Mr. Wiggins' s'prise."

As soon as lunch was over, the family hurried outside to their new station wagon. Before long Mr. Bobbsey was driving along the broad highway leading from Lakeport near the shore of Lake Metoka. Fifteen minutes later he turned off onto a dirt road which led to Mr. Wiggins' lovely farm on the lake shore.

"There's the house," Mrs. Bobbsey said, pointing to an old-fashioned farm home with a modern white barn behind it.

As Mr. Bobbsey turned into the lane Mr. Wiggins opened the porch door and hurried down the steps. He was slender in build and had a rosy, tanned complexion. He wore khaki trousers and shirt, and red suspenders. A straw hat sat back on his bald head.

"Glad to see you, Dick!" he smiled, shaking hands with Mr. Bobbsey. "And you, too, Mary," he said to the twins' mother.

Mr. and Mrs. Bobbsey returned the greeting and introduced their children. They liked Mr. Wiggins immediately. Although elderly, he moved briskly and had a merry twinkle in his eyes.

"This dad of yours is a wonderful fellow," the farmer said. "He helped me build that dairy barn over yonder when the old one burned down."

"What's in the barn?" Flossie asked.

"You come with me and I'll show you."

The twins ran ahead of the grownups and reached the big double door first. Looking inside, they saw a row of cows in stalls on one side and on the other a row of goats.

As a loud *moo* was heard, Flossie giggled. "Oh, it's a menagerie farm," she said.

Farmer Wiggins, coming up, laughed and said, "Well, it is sort of that."

He explained that he specialized in cattle

breeding and also had milking cows and goats.

"I have something special to show you children," he said, chuckling. "Your mother and dad have the same thing."

"What's that?" asked Bert.

"Twins!"

"Really?" Nan exclaimed.

Flossie asked, "Are they look-alike twins like us?"

Mr. Wiggins laughed. "They're right over here," he said, leading them through the barn.

In a separate, straw-floored stall stood twin calves that looked exactly alike.

"Oh, aren't they cute!" Nan cried.

"Cute and frisky!" Mr. Wiggins told her.

"I'd like to ride one," said Freddie, "and be a cowboy!"

"Let's do it then," the farmer agreed. As he led the calves out of the barn, Nan asked what their names were.

"Cindy and Mindy. Now who else wants to ride?"

"I'd like to," said Bert.

"And me!" cried Nan and Flossie together.

The older twins had rides first and held on tightly as the calves ran around the barnyard.

Then the farmer helped Flossie to get on Mindy's back and Mr. Bobbsey helped Freddie on Cindy. For a while the animals walked around slowly. Finally Mindy grew tired of this pace and began to walk faster. Then she broke into a little trot. Flossie bounced up and down on the animal's back.

"Help, I'm falling off!" she said. "Mindy's s-slippery!"

As there was nothing to hold onto, Flossie slid off the animal's back and landed in a pile of straw alongside the barn!

"Ha, ha," laughed Freddie. "I'm a better rider." But he had no sooner said this when *zip* —he fell off Cindy's back the same way and landed *kerplunk!* on the ground!

Though he scraped an elbow, Freddie gamely

brushed himself off and helped the farmer lead the calves back to their stall.

"Mr. Wiggins," Bert said as they walked from the barn. "Please tell us the surprise."

"I wondered when you'd ask that. Come on! I'll show it to you."

He led the way to the lake shore. Reaching the water, he pointed.

"Look over there!"

"A little ferryboat!" Bert cried. "A real ferryboat!"

"Why, sure enough, it is," Mr. Bobbsey said, his face breaking into a big grin.

The children raced over to get a better view of the craft. They had never seen a ferryboat on Lake Metoka before. The boat had a small cabin, with a pilot house above it, and a deck that ran all the way around the cabin. The ferry was in need of paint but was very sturdy looking.

"May we get on it, please?" Freddie asked. "I love boats."

"Of course, and maybe we'll take a ride," the farmer said. "But first, there's a question I want to ask you twins." Mr. Wiggins' eyes were twinkling.

"What is it?" Bert asked eagerly.

Farmer Wiggins smiled at the twins and said, "How would you like to own this ferryboat?"

CHAPTER V

GOAT OVERBOARD!

MR. WIGGINS' offer of the old ferryboat caused the twins to shout with glee.

"Our own little ferryboat!" Nan cried excitedly. "Oh, I can't believe it!"

The farmer turned to Mr. Bobbsey. "The boat is yours if you want it. What do you say, Dick?"

"I think you're very generous," the twins' father replied. "All I can say is, thank you, Homer."

"Yes, indeed," Mrs. Bobbsey added. "This is a wonderful gift."

"You're the nicest man ever!" Flossie said, suddenly throwing her arms about Mr. Wiggins.

"Where did you get the ferryboat?" Bert asked, while the other twins ran out on the dock to inspect their prize.

The farmer said he had bought the boat second-hand long ago to ferry his cattle across the water. "See that small island over yonder?" he asked. "There's a wonderful rich pasture on it. My cows and goats have been eating that grass for many years. This little ferryboat has been carrying them back and forth."

"What kind of engine runs it?" Bert asked.

"A diesel," Mr. Wiggins replied. "Works fine and it isn't expensive to run." After a pause, he added, "I'm sorry the animals' hoofs have scuffed the boat up so much. But a coat of fresh paint will do wonders."

"May we go aboard?" Freddie requested as he and his twin neared the gangplank.

"Go right ahead," the farmer said. "In fact, I must make one more trip to the island to bring my herds back. They'll be sold tomorrow."

Bert, remembering Mr. Wiggins' words about a possible ride, asked hopefully when he would make the last trip. "Right away," the farmer answered. "Would you like to come with me?"

The shout of enthusiasm from the Bobbseys was enough to tell Mr. Wiggins that they would love to go for a ride in their own little ferryboat.

When they were aboard, Mr. Wiggins showed the children how to pull up the gangplank. Then he climbed the stairs to the little pilot house and started the engine.

The propeller churned up white foam in the water. Smiling, Mr. Wiggins pulled a cord and the deep-sounding horn went *Boop! Boop!* The farmer turned the big steering wheel slightly and the ferryboat set off across the lake.

Freddie was the first one to visit the pilot house. He stood alongside Mr. Wiggins and said wistfully, "May I try steering it a few minutes? If this is our boat now, I ought to learn how."

"Of course you may. Here, take the wheel and hold her on a steady course in line with that big tree on the island."

Freddie had to stand on his tiptoes to look through the window at a tall oak tree which towered above the other trees. Then, by turning the wheel first a little to the left and then to the right, he kept the boat on an even course.

"May I try it too?" came Flossie's voice as she climbed the stairs to the pilot house.

"Certainly." Freddie gave up the wheel to his sister, and Mr. Wiggins added, "Easy does it, Flossie."

But Flossie was so excited that she pulled hard with her right hand. Immediately the boat began to head for the shore.

"Hey, we're going the wrong way!" Freddie shouted.

"Pull the wheel the other way," Mr. Wiggins directed calmly. When Flossie did this, the boat went straight ahead once more.

It was not long before Bert and Nan also asked if they might steer the ferry, and then Mrs. Bobbsey walked up the steps to the pilot house.

"How about letting me try, too?" she asked, smiling.

"Hurray, Mother's a ferryboat pilot!" Freddie shouted.

Mrs. Bobbsey headed straight for the island. This was as large as a city block, with a sandy beach and lots of grass and trees. Not far back from the shore stood cows and goats contentedly munching grass.

As the ferryboat drew close to the island's dock, Mr. Wiggins took over the wheel. He cut the engine and let the boat drift in.

Bert and Nan quickly put the gangplank down while Freddie and Flossie helped their father tie the ferry securely. Then the twins ran onto the island.

"What a lovely place this is!" said Nan, looking around. She added poetically, "It's just like a green emerald set in sparkling water."

Her twin was not as interested in the beauty of the spot as he was in helping to get the cattle aboard. "May we help you with the roundup?" he asked Mr. Wiggins.

"Thank you, yes," the farmer replied. "I'll need help. I let my hired man go yesterday."

As the Bobbseys approached the cattle, they could hear the mooing of the cows and the bleating of the goats.

"Poor things, you're going on your last boat ride," Flossie told the animals.

The farmer assured the children that the herds would be in good hands even though they could no longer graze on the island.

"Suppose all you twins help me round up the goats and cows now."

There were six goats and twelve cows. What a lively time the twins had herding them toward the beach! Every once in a while, one of the goats would dash away and have to be chased back with the others.

The cows, meanwhile, plodded slowly toward the dock, their bells ringing as they tossed their heads back and forth.

"They're all here, Mr. Wiggins," Nan said proudly.

Then came the job of coaxing the cows and goats across the gangplank, then onto the deck of the ferryboat.

"This is just like an ark," Flossie said, giggling, "and your name should be Mr. Noah," she told the farmer.

"All the animals are aboard!" Bert shouted finally. "Shall we raise the gangplank?"

"Heave to, mate!" the farmer ordered, sounding like a real sea captain.

When everything was in readiness, Mr. Wiggins beckoned to Bert. "How would you like to back the boat off and head home?"

Bert grinned and climbed into the pilot house with the farmer. He pulled a lever which made

"You're going on your last boat ride,"
Flossie told the animals

the propellers go in reverse. Slowly the little ferryboat backed away from the dock. When it was far enough out, Bert reversed the propellers and turned the boat around in a large arc. Flossie climbed up the stairway and stood beside him tooting the funny horn.

"Here we go with our ark!" Freddie called as his parents looked around with amusement.

Mr. Bobbsey called up to Farmer Wiggins, "I'll have to arrange for a dock before we can take the ferryboat away."

"I know where there are two docks, Dad," Bert spoke up. "They're fairly near your lumberyard. They belong to the Ace Boat Company and the Lakeport Warehouse. No one seems to use them."

"You're right, son," Mr. Bobbsey said. "Perhaps we can rent one. We'll see when we get home." He walked up the stairs to take a turn at the wheel.

Nan, meanwhile, had been talking with her mother. "What fun we're going to have on Lake Metoka this summer! We can take lots of trips back and forth with our friends. We could even bring picnic lunches and stay out all day."

"Yes," Mrs. Bobbsey agreed. "You children will surely have a very happy summer on your new boat. Mr. Wiggins certainly knows what children like."

By this time Flossie had grown tired of play-

ing with the horn and came running down the
steps from the pilot house. Flossie tapped Freddie on the shoulder and raced away.

"You're it! Try to catch me!" she cried.

Freddie ran after her, dashing from one part
of the boat to another. He did not catch her, and
the racing caused the cows and goats to become
excited and move from side to side. This made
the boat list one way, then the other. It seemed
as if the ferry might capsize at any moment.

"Oo!" cried Flossie.

"Children, stop!" Mrs. Bobbsey called to
them. "You're frightening the animals! We'll
have an accident!"

"Yes, Mother," Flossie said, and obediently
stopped playing the game.

In a short time the cows and goats quieted
down and stood placid once more. But one young
goat kept turning her head around and pawing
the deck.

Freddie noticed this and called up to Mr.
Wiggins, "There's one goat here that won't stand
still!"

"Oh, that's Tilly. She's always nervous," the
farmer replied. Turning to Bert, he said, "I'll
take over, son, if you'll be so kind as to get a
piece of rope in the cabin. Tie Tilly up with
that."

Bert hurried off to find the rope while
Freddie put his arms around the goat's neck.

The animal struggled to duck under the rail.

"You hold still!" Freddie commanded. "Bert, hurry! Quick!"

Bert dashed from the cabin and across the deck just as the goat gave a sudden lurch to free herself from Freddie's grasp. Before the older boy could get the rope around Tilly, she slid under the rail.

Splash! The goat tumbled headfirst into the water.

"Goat overboard! Goat overboard!" Freddie cried, jumping up and down as the animal disappeared.

All the children ran to the rail, shouting in alarm. A moment later Tilly's head came to the surface and she began to swim.

"She's going home by herself," Flossie said, giggling.

But this was not Tilly's idea. She set off down the lake.

"You're going the wrong way!" called Flossie.

"Stop, please stop!" Nan shouted to the goat.

"Come back!" Freddie pleaded.

But Tilly paid no attention. She seemed to be enjoying her freedom and continued swimming away from the ferryboat.

"I'll get her!" Bert shouted.

Quickly stripping off his shirt and moccasins, he plunged into the lake. With strong strokes he started swimming toward the runaway goat.

CHAPTER VI

A GYPSY GRANDMOTHER

"CATCH the goat, Bert!" Freddie shouted from the deck of the ferryboat.

But Tilly, hearing the boy in the water behind her, swam all the faster. Becoming frightened, she jerked her neck from side to side trying to see him.

Bert, in a great burst of speed, caught up with the animal and grabbed her tail. Then he pushed her around to head for the shore. But Tilly, not understanding, started floundering in circles while giving soft, whining bleats.

"Okay," said the boy soothingly.

He released his hold on the animal and swam shoulder to shoulder with her, nudging the goat toward the farm. Whenever she turned in the wrong direction, Bert gently guided her the right way.

From the ferryboat everyone called encour-

agement. Mr. Wiggins, at the wheel, slowed
down and kept pace with the swimmers in case
either of them should tire and need help.

But both Bert and Tilly made the journey
with little effort. They reached shallow water
five minutes later. When the goat's forefeet
touched the shore, she waded to the beach, then
dashed toward the barn.

"She's saved!" cried Flossie happily.

"Yes," said Nan, proud of her twin brother.

Bert sat on the beach to wait for the ferryboat
to land. The gangplank was lowered, and Nan
and Freddie helped tie the boat to its mooring.

Clomp! clomp! clomp! The cows and goats
began to stomp off the boat. Mr. Wiggins and
the children drove them into the big barn.

After the animals were secure in their proper
stanchions, the farmer said, "Come with me,
Bert. I'll find dry clothes for you at the house."

The boy followed him and put on a dry shirt and trousers. The shirt hung loosely on Bert's shoulders, the sleeves were too long, and the trousers had to be rolled up. This made everyone laugh, and Freddie added:

"Put on an old hat and you'll look like a scarecrow!"

When the joking died down, Nan said, "Mr. Wiggins, who owns the island?"

"I do," the farmer replied. "It's part of my property."

"Are you selling it with the farm?" Nan pressed.

The man nodded. "Yes, I am, but the new owner will not use it as a pasture. I don't know what he intends to do with it."

Nan hesitated, then said, "Do you suppose the new owner will use the island right away?"

Mr. Wiggins replied that the buyer would not be taking possession of the property for a couple of months because he was going out of town on a trip.

Nan's face brightened. "Could we rent your island until the new owner returns?" she asked.

Mr. and Mrs. Bobbsey looked at their daughter in surprise. They wondered why she wanted to rent a lonely island in the center of the lake.

Mr. Wiggins, however, gave an amused chuckle. "Rent it?" he said. "Why, you Bobbseys may use it free. What do you want to do with it, Nan—fix it up as a pirate's hideout?"

"Oh, I love to play pirate!" Freddie interrupted, throwing out his chest. "Flossie, you can be my prisoner and I'll make you walk the plank!"

Nan smiled and stated that a pirate's hideout was not what she had in mind.

"I have another idea," she said, her eyes sparkling in anticipation. "Maybe we could fix the island up as a picnic ground and take people out there in our ferryboat. We'd charge for the trip and what we collect could be added to the school fair money."

"That's a swell idea!" Bert said.

"And I could ride back and forth on the boat all day," Freddie beamed. "Let's do it!"

The twins' parents agreed that Nan's idea was a novel one and should make money. They gave their consent and the children shouted in glee.

"Now we must return home," said Mrs. Bobbsey. "Mr. Wiggins, you've certainly made this a happy day for all of us."

The twins were so excited about Nan's scheme that they all hurried back to the beach for one more look at the wonderful ferryboat.

"This will be keen!" Bert exclaimed, looking forward to a summer of boat trips on the lake. "I'm going to tell Charlie Mason about it as soon as I get back."

Charlie was Bert's age and one of his closest friends. All the children were eager to tell their playmates about Nan's great idea, but Flossie's face clouded.

"There's someone we can't tell," she said.

"Who's that?" Bert asked.

"Danny Rugg!" said the little girl. "If he hears about our plan, he may do something to spoil it."

"Flossie's right," Nan agreed. "We won't tell Danny until we're actually taking people to the island on picnics."

Everyone promised that he would not breathe a word to the bully or any of his pals. Again the family thanked the farmer for his wonderful gift and they started back to Lakeport.

When Dinah heard the news, she threw up her hands. "Lands sakes! A ferryboat! You children had your own little railroad and now this boat. Goodness gracious, it wouldn't surprise me to see Freddie walk in with a real fire engine one of these days!"

"Wouldn't that be great!" cried Freddie.

Sam also was interested in the project. "Will you children take me to the island?" he asked, smiling so broadly that all his fine white teeth showed. "I heard tell about some mighty big catfish over there. Maybe I could catch a couple for our dinner sometime."

Bert said they would try this some day, but

first the Bobbseys must find a dock in Lakeport for the ferryboat.

"We'll do some scouting around after church tomorrow," Mr. Bobbsey suggested.

The next afternoon he drove the family along the shore road and made inquiries about the two docks near the Bobbsey lumberyard. But both had been rented for the summer. Several other docks located along the shore were too small for the ferryboat.

"I'll make some inquiries around town tomorrow morning," Mr. Bobbsey promised as they finally gave up the search.

After school the next day Bert phoned his father. "Sorry, son, I didn't have any luck," Mr. Bobbsey said. "And there's another problem," he added. "You'll need an older person for a skipper on these trips back and forth to the island."

Bert was downcast for a moment. Then he said hopefully, "Dad, I'm sure you can find someone. And I'll start looking for a dock."

When Flossie heard the problems, tears rolled down her cheeks. "You—you mean we can't keep our present?" she wailed.

"Of course we can," Bert assured her. "We'll fix everything up." He went for his bike and rode to Charlie Mason's. "Come and help me find a dock for our ferryboat," he said to Charlie.

"Sure thing. Wait'll I tell Mother where I'm going." Bert's good-looking, brown-haired friend had been keen about the island plan the minute he had heard it that morning.

Meanwhile, Nan and the younger twins played around the house. Snap's long white fur needed grooming so Freddie started this work. Flossie sat under a big tree cutting out paper dolls. Nan was just about to pick a bouquet for the dining-room table when she noticed a girl coming up their front walk.

"Tara!" Nan called, hurrying to her friend's side. "I'm so glad you came."

Tara O'Toole was dressed very differently from the way she had been on the day she had told fortunes. Instead of the mantilla, her shiny black hair hung to her shoulders, and short, curly bangs covered her forehead where the gold coin had been. She wore a flowered dress much like Nan's in place of the gypsy skirt and blouse.

"Oh, Tara, don't you dress like a gypsy all the time?" Flossie asked, running over to the two girls.

Freddie, too, dashed up to greet their young visitor. "Can't you tell fortunes any more?" he asked in a disappointed voice.

Tara smiled at the small twins, her lovely dark eyes twinkling.

"I only wear my costume for special things— like telling fortunes at the school fair," she said.

"I'm an American, just as you are. Besides, I'm only half gypsy."

She reminded the others that it was Madame Lene, her grandmother in Spain, who was a real gypsy. "But I can still read palms, even in my everyday dress," she assured Freddie.

"That's good," said the little boy.

"I came to tell you I've just heard some wonderful news," Tara went on.

"What is it?" the three Bobbseys chorused excitedly.

"My gypsy grandmother," Tara replied, "is coming to visit us!"

"All the way from Spain?" Flossie asked, wide-eyed.

As Tara nodded, Freddie piped up eagerly, "Is she coming on a boat?" He was thinking how grand it would be to travel such a long way by water.

"Yes," Tara replied, "and Uncle Romaine is coming with Madame Lene. He's my mother's younger brother. I've only seen pictures of him. He's very handsome and is a bullfighter."

At this announcement Freddie came close to Tara. "A bullfighter!" he cried. "Oh, I want to see him!"

"You will," Tara promised. "And my famous grandmother too. She's known all over Spain for her marvelous fortunetelling."

As Flossie's and Nan's eyes brightened, Tara

went on, "And she's bringing her beautiful mantilla, too."

"Is it as pretty as yours?" Nan asked her friend.

"Oh, yes. It's much prettier. It is the most gorgeous in all the world."

"Then it must be priceless," said Nan.

Tara nodded, then explained that her grandmother's valuable headpiece was very, very old. Besides being studded with gold pieces, it also contained diamonds and other precious gems.

"Are the gold pieces like the one on your mantilla?" Nan wanted to know.

"Yes. The coin on mine came from Madame Lene's," Tara said.

"Your grandmother's headdress sounds like something out of a fairy tale," Flossie spoke up.

"I hope we can see it some day," said Nan dreamily.

Tara promised her friends that they would see the mantilla, saying she would invite them over to her house when her relatives arrived from Spain.

"And now I should go," Tara added.

"Oh, no," Flossie pleaded, tugging the girl's hand. "Please show us how to read palms!"

The gypsy girl paused. "All right," she agreed.

CHAPTER VII

SECRET PLANS

FREDDIE, Flossie, and Nan sat down with Tara on the grass under a maple tree.

"Is it hard to read palms?" Nan asked her.

"No, not really. But there's a lot to remember. Well, I'll show you a little."

Holding Nan's right palm upward, Tara said that there were seven main lines and many smaller ones in everyone's hand. "Each line means something special," she explained.

Flossie jumped up. "Please wait a minute," she said. "I want to copy down the lines." She ran into the house and soon returned with a pad and pencil. Then she told Freddie to lay his hand on the pad and she outlined the fingers.

"Ready?" asked Tara, and pointed to a line which ran across the top of Nan's palm. "This is the *heart line*," she said. "One thing it tells is whether you are a friendly person or someone who likes to play alone."

Flossie busily sketched in the line as Tara continued, "And the *head line,* right beneath it, shows what you like and how you think. See it?"

The children nodded. Then Tara ran her finger down a crease in Nan's palm which ended at the base of her thumb.

"Here is your *life line,* Nan. It tells me that you will live for many years and always be healthy."

Nan was pleased to hear this. Her friend pointed out other lines—those for health, marriage, fate, and the one telling whether a person would lead a successful, happy life.

Flossie sighed. "There's so much to remember," she protested, "I've forgotten half of it already."

"And I've only begun to tell you!" Tara said, laughing. "So many other things are important. The way you shake hands, the shape of your fingers, and the color and depth of the lines all mean something."

Just then, Freddie, who had been taking in the lesson wide-eyed, stood up. "Come on, Flossie," he cried, "let's you and me practice palm reading on Dinah and Sam."

They dashed inside the house and found Dinah seated at the kitchen table paring apples.

Sam, who had left the lumberyard early, had just come home.

"We're fortunetellers!" Freddie announced. "We'll tell your fortunes for an apple, Dinah."

Dinah chuckled. "That sounds like a good trade." She laid her paring knife in the bowl, then wiped her hands on her checkered apron. "Now just what's in store for old Dinah?" she asked, holding her hands toward the twins.

"The right hand is the one that really counts," Flossie said. "Hmmm, let me see!" She glanced from the sheet of paper to Dinah's hand. "Your heart line's bee-yoo-ti-ful!" she cried, studying the straight, unbroken line.

"My wife sure *is* good-hearted!" Sam said affectionately. "Her heart's made of solid gold!"

Freddie agreed. "Dinah makes cakes 'n' pies for us all the time," he said.

Dinah grinned and urged Flossie to go on. "This is exciting!" she exclaimed.

"Oh, you're going to live a long, long time," Flossie told her as she traced Dinah's life line. "At least a hundred years!"

The kindly woman burst into laughter. "My, that's sure a long time," she said. "But if I do, I hope I live every minute of it with you Bobbseys!" Then she added, "What's my fate, honey child? Do you see any black cats coming my way?"

"Only Snoop," Flossie assured her, referring to the family pet. "You really have a good fate, Dinah."

"Now that's just wonderful!" Dinah remarked and thanked the young fortuneteller. "How about telling Sam's?" she suggested, starting to pare apples again.

"Let me," said Freddie, and looked closely into Sam's large hand. After studying it for a while, Freddie glanced up. "Where's your other head, Sam?"

"My other head?" Sam cried, startled. "What do you mean, boy?"

"You have two head lines," Freddie said. "Look, it's right here, isn't it, Flossie?"

His sister had to agree that Sam indeed had two head lines. "That's awful funny," said Freddie, puzzled.

"Yes, but it doesn't mean that Sam has two heads, Freddie," said his twin. "It just means Sam is extra smart!"

"I don't know about that." Dinah shook her head. "He left half the grocery order at the store this morning. And he's wearing socks that don't match!"

"Hush, Dinah!" her husband protested. "I want to find out more about myself. Go on, Freddie."

The little boy told Sam that he was generous

and good-natured. "You are married too, Sam," Freddie added importantly. This made Dinah laugh so heartily that she nearly dropped the bowl of apples.

"Please cross our palms with an apple now," begged Flossie, as the fortunetelling ended.

Dinah pared two apples, split them down the middle to remove the seeds, and placed a half in each child's hand.

"Thank you, Dinah," the twins chorused and skipped out the back door munching the fruit.

Waggo raced up to meet them and stood on his hind legs begging for a bit of apple. Flossie gave him one as Freddie said:

"Let's tell Waggo's fortune."

Although it was hard to hold Waggo still long enough to look at his right front paw, the twins finally succeeded.

"Tara was right—he doesn't have any lines like we do," Freddie said, disappointed.

"Maybe that's 'cause he walks on them all the time," Flossie guessed.

Seeing the dog prance about on his hind legs gave the little girl an idea. She dashed into the house and returned a few minutes later with a battered old hat and a short cane which she had won at the school fair.

As her brother looked on curiously, Flossie put the hat on Waggo's head and the cane in his

"That's a wonderful trick!" Freddie said

mouth. Then she snapped her fingers to make the fox terrier walk around on his hind legs.

"That's a wonderful trick!" Freddie cried approvingly and clapped his hands.

"I think so, too! And I know where Waggo could earn some money doing it," said Flossie.

"Where?"

"On the island. Waggo could do tricks and we could charge people to see him," she said.

Freddie thought this was a fine idea and raced over to tell Nan and Tara about it.

"That's grand!" said Tara. Nan had just told her about the ferryboat. "Maybe you could have other acts, too," she suggested.

"Why not tell fortunes, Tara?" Freddie exclaimed. "You can use the same tent."

Looking pleased, Tara agreed to do this. "And I'm sure all your other friends will want to help," she said.

"Let's call them and have a meeting!" Nan cried excitedly.

The two girls hurried into the house and made calls to Nellie Parks, Grace Levine, and several other girls and boys in their class.

Soon the children began arriving at the Bobbseys' back yard. Nellie Parks came first. She was followed by Grace Levine, twelve, who had straight, shiny dark hair. Several other boys and girls joined them shortly.

"Tell us what this meeting's all about!" begged Grace. "I'm terribly curious!"

"Me, too," said a red-haired, freckle-faced boy. "Give us the scoop."

Nan laughed and suggested that everyone sit in a circle so she could be heard better. Then she outlined their hopes for raising school money with trips in the ferryboat and little shows and entertainment on the island.

"That's marvelous!" Grace cried.

All the children were enthusiastic and could hardly wait to begin the project. Just then, Dinah, who had seen the little crowd in the back yard, brought out cookies and grape juice.

"But we must keep our plan a secret from Danny Rugg," Nan warned, as the children thanked Dinah and began to eat.

"And from Jack Westley, too," Freddie put in. Jack was Danny's special friend, and together the two boys got into all kinds of mischief.

"I'd like to ask Danny to help, because he's in our class," Nan explained. "But I'm afraid he'd only cause trouble."

"He sure would," agreed Nellie Parks.

"Okay, mum's the word," Grace promised, and the other children nodded in agreement.

"Just let us know what we can do," said the red-haired boy, whose name was Bill.

One by one the children said good-by and went home. Tara was the last to leave. As Nan stood waving to her friend, Mrs. Bobbsey walked out the kitchen door into the yard.

"Dinah tells me you've had company," said the twins' mother, who had been out shopping.

After Nan, Flossie, and Freddie told her all about their meeting, she smiled.

"Since today was the last day of school," said Mrs. Bobbsey, "you'll have plenty of time now to work on your wonderful project. And I know that you'll have a lot of fun this summer. It'll be good for all you twins to be out in the fresh air and sunshine."

"But how will we get to the island, Mother?" Freddie asked. "We haven't found anybody to help us steer our ferryboat."

"Maybe Sam could do it," Flossie suggested.

Her mother reminded the little girl that Sam would be busy working at the lumberyard and helping around their home.

"Gee whiz," said Freddie, "I still don't see why we need another pilot when I'm around." His face brightened as he added, "I know, Mother—you could be the pilot and I could help you!"

Mrs. Bobbsey laughed and admitted she would enjoy this. "But keeping house is a full-time job as it is," she said.

His mother had been thinking about the pilot problem and now she thought she had an answer.

"Maybe Mr. Wiggins will have some free time this summer to help you run the boat," she said. "If it would be more convenient for him, I'd be glad to have him stay here with us until the playground project is finished. Would you children like that?"

"Oh, yes!" they all cried, and Flossie added, "That's a swell idea, Mother!"

"Please, may we phone him right away and ask?" Freddie pleaded.

"Go ahead."

Beaming, Nan rushed hopefully to the telephone in the hall.

CHAPTER VIII

A BAD ACCIDENT

QUICKLY finding Mr. Wiggins' number in the telephone book, Nan dialed the call. When the farmer answered, she told him all about the plans for their island adventure.

"Well, that sounds splendid," he said. "I've been wondering whether the Bobbsey twins were going ahead with the idea of running the ferry-boat to the island," he chuckled.

"Yes, indeed," said Nan. "But we need some-one older than we are to be in charge of the boat. Could you possibly do it for us?" Nan now mentioned her mother's suggestion that he visit them.

"I'd be pleased to help," said Mr. Wiggins. "I'm getting kind of lonesome now that I'm retired. This will give me something to do until I move away."

He added that he hoped they had found a dock, for his own was too far from Lakeport to be practical. Sighing, Nan told him Bert and a friend were out now trying to find one.

"Let's hope they have good luck," said Mr. Wiggins. "Well, let me know when you want me to come." Then he and Nan said good-by.

Unfortunately Bert and Charlie so far had not been successful. They had started their trip by pedaling along the shore road out of town. But though the boys had located several docks, they were either the wrong size or not for rent.

"Let's ride back into town," Bert now suggested.

"But all the docks there are in use," Charlie replied, looking discouraged.

"We might be more lucky on the other side of Lakeport," came the reply.

Turning their bicycles around, the boys sped back along the road. Hearing sounds behind them, Bert glanced back over his shoulder.

"Say, Charlie, did you notice those two fellows on bikes behind us?"

Charlie slowed down and looked back. "No, I didn't," he said. "I wonder who they are?"

"Maybe they're trying to catch up to us."

"Then let's wait and ask them what they want, Bert."

The two boys slid off their bicycle seats, straddled the crossbars, and waited.

But the mysterious riders stopped just as abruptly and remained in the road. When Bert and

Charlie set off again, however, the other boys did likewise. They remained far enough behind so the two in front could not make out their faces.

"Those fellows are spying on us," Bert said, annoyed. "I'm sure of it."

"Tell you what," said Charlie. "Let's hide behind that big tree at the bend in the road. As they ride past, we can see who they are."

Bert grinned in agreement and the two boys pedaled close to the side of the road. When they came to the tree, they jumped from their bikes, dragged them into the bushes, and lay flat on the ground.

Presently they heard the other wheels approaching. One of the riders said in a hoarse voice, "Ha, they don't know who we are!"

"You're right, Jack, we've fooled 'em!" said the other.

Bert and Charlie recognized both boys' voices —they belonged to Danny Rugg and his pal Jack Westley!

Nudging Charlie, Bert called out to them, "Having a good time?"

Startled, Danny and Jack jerked their heads to one side and immediately got off their bikes. As Bert and Charlie stood up and pulled their bicycles erect, the other boys looked amazed.

But Danny's expression instantly turned to a sneer. "What are you hiding there for? Think you're groundhogs?"

"Well, at least we're not spies!" Charlie retorted.

"Who's a spy?" growled Jack. "We were just out for a ride."

"Don't make me laugh!" said Bert. "You were following us."

At this, Danny Rugg leaned his bike against the tree and confronted Bert. "I'll punch you for saying I don't tell the truth!" he shouted.

"If you want to make something of it, go ahead!" Bert said firmly.

"Hit him, Danny!" Jack urged.

But Bert's angry face caused Danny to back down. Glaring at Jack, he said, "If you're so anxious to fight Bert, why don't you do it?"

Jack licked his lips and said nothing for fear that Danny would pounce on him instead.

"Okay, okay!" Danny said angrily. "Anyway, I was only trying to help you, Bert."

"That's a joke!" Charlie exclaimed. "When did you ever try to help any of the Bobbseys?"

A nasty grin came over Danny Rugg's face. "Well, Jack and I were only trying to find a dock for their old ferryboat."

Bert and Charlie gasped. "How did you learn about our boat?" Bert asked with a sinking feeling.

"We get around," Danny said smugly, enjoying Bert's dismay that he had learned the

Bobbseys' secret. "Well, go find a dock all by yourselves. And when you do, I hope it caves in!"

He and Jack jumped on their bikes and rode off, leaving Bert and Charlie staring at each other in bewilderment.

"Who told him?" Bert said, as he watched the boys disappear down the road.

Charlie suggested that perhaps Flossie or Freddie might have told the secret to some young friend who had not kept it. Bert doubted this, but said nothing. Then he and Charlie started glumly back to Lakeport.

"Say, I have an idea, Bert," Charlie said after they had ridden through town and were starting along the far shore. "My aunt Sue Smith lives on the lakefront. She has a dock. Maybe we could use hers."

"It's worth a try, I guess," said Bert hopefully.

With Charlie in the lead the boys pedaled down one street and up another.

"Let's take this back alley for a short cut," Charlie suggested, as they rode down a lane flanked on both sides by rows of garages.

Bert was the first to notice a rope lying on the ground across the width of the narrow alley. But before he had a chance to think twice about it, the rope suddenly sprang up waist high.

"Hey, what's this?" Charlie shouted. He and Bert both tried to stop, but their bicycles plowed into the rope.

Being nearly taut, it caused them to stop short, and both boys fell headlong into the dirt! Their bicycles skidded along the ground beside them.

"Are you hurt, Charlie?" Bert exclaimed as he sprang to his feet to help his friend.

"Just shaken up a bit, that's all," Charlie replied. He rose and dusted his clothes. "Who did that, Bert?"

"I don't know, Charlie, but two boys were holding that rope. I caught a glimpse of them as I spilled. Do you know anyone who lives around here?"

Charlie thought for a moment, then snapped his fingers. "Yes! Jack Westley lives on the next block."

"He does?"

"Sure, and I'll bet he and Danny are the ones who tripped us. Of all the mean tricks!"

Charlie and Bert tried to find the other two boys, but they were not at Jack's house.

"We'll attend to them later," Bert said. "Let's go see your aunt, Charlie."

After examining their bicycles to be sure that no parts were broken, the boys made their way to Mrs. Smith's home. She had a neat cottage by the waterfront and a sturdy dock which extended out about twenty-five feet into Lake Metoka.

"Boy, that's a dandy!" said Bert. "Just what we need."

"We'll go in and I'll ask my aunt," Charlie offered, and they mounted the front steps of the cottage.

They were greeted at the door by a friendly middle-aged woman. She was very pretty, with wavy, blond hair and a warm smile.

"Why, Charlie," she said, giving her nephew a hug. "It's so nice to see you."

"Aunt Sue, this is Bert Bobbsey," Charlie said, and Mrs. Smith extended her hand.

"I'm glad to know you, Bert. Won't you boys come in?" she said. "And how about a piece of cake and a bottle of pop?"

The boys grinned at each other, then thanked Aunt Sue and said they would be delighted. While they were seated in the living room, enjoying the cake, Charlie spoke up. "Aunt Sue, would you be willing to let the Bobbseys keep their ferryboat at your dock?" he asked.

"Ferryboat!" Aunt Sue cried. She looked so startled that Bert and Charlie were afraid she would not consent.

"It would be for only a short time while we run a project on the island," Bert said and quickly explained the whole story.

Mrs. Smith smiled. "I'll be glad to let you use my dock," she said. "I have a little motorboat— really a large rowboat with an outboard motor— but I can keep it on one side of the dock with my smaller rowboat. You use the end for your ferryboat."

The boys were so happy to hear this good news that they refused a second helping of cake in order to hurry home and tell the other Bobbseys and their friends.

What excitement there was that evening for the twins! Bert and Nan between them had solved the two problems. Now the island project could begin.

Mr. Bobbsey and all the twins called on the school principal after supper to tell him about the fund-raising idea. Mr. Tetlow was very pleased and said he hoped they would make a lot of money for the school fund.

Before going to bed that evening Nan phoned to Mr. Wiggins, saying they were ready to get the ferryboat. He was happy to hear this and said he would be glad to see them the following day.

Since Mr. Bobbsey would be busy the next morning, he told Sam to drive the twins and Charlie Mason to Mr. Wiggins' farm. When they were ready to leave in the station wagon they found Waggo already aboard. He refused to get out, so they took him along.

When they arrived at the farm Mr. Wiggins had two suitcases packed and said he was looking forward to a visit at the Bobbseys'. After Bert had introduced him to Sam and Charlie, Mr. Wiggins said, "I reckon you youngsters would like to go back with me aboard the ferryboat."

"Oh, yes!" the twins cried.

Sam grinned. "Waggo and I will drive the car home and tell Mr. Bobbsey where you are."

But the fox terrier had other ideas. He ran aboard the ferry and barked happily. "I guess he wants to ride with us," said Flossie, and Sam told her this would be all right.

The children waved to the kindly Negro as he drove off, then hurried to the dock to show Charlie Mason their new ferryboat.

"It's keen!" Charlie cried as everyone hurried aboard.

The small twins led Charlie throughout the boat while Bert carried Mr. Wiggins' bags into the cabin. The farmer took over the wheel and started the engine. After Bert and Charlie had untied the boat, Freddie climbed to the pilot house and blew the horn.

"Here we come, everybody!" he shouted. "This is the Bobbsey Special!"

It took nearly an hour to make the trip to Lakeport. During this time the children shared the box lunch that Mr. Wiggins had brought aboard.

"Land ho!" Bert shouted as they finished eating and came in sight of the Lakeport shoreline.

"There's my aunt's place over there." Charlie pointed and guided Mr. Wiggins toward the Smiths' dock. But as they drew close to it, the children cried in dismay.

A string of rowboats was tied up at the end of the dock and on both sides!

"We can't land," said Farmer Wiggins in bewilderment.

CHAPTER IX

A SCHEME BACKFIRES

DISMAY showed in the faces of the five children when the ferryboat could not land.

"What could have gone wrong?" Charlie cried. "Aunt Sue said—"

"I'll bet this is more of Danny and Jack's work!" Bert interrupted, frowning.

Charlie counted the boats. "There are ten of them and only two belong to my aunt."

"What'll we do? Anybody have an idea?" Mr. Wiggins asked, looking down from the pilot house.

"I have," said Nan, who was standing beside him. She blew the boat's horn several times.

In a few moments Mrs. Smith hurried outdoors to see what was causing the commotion. Charlie introduced the girls and Mr. Wiggins, then told their predicament.

Aunt Sue came to the edge of the dock and looked down. Reading the names on the rowboats, she said, "Why, these belong to my various neighbors. Now *who* tied them up here?"

"We think we know," called Bert, adding, "If the boats don't belong here, then we'll take them away and the ferry can land."

"Yes," said Aunt Sue. "I'll come out to you in my motorboat. You older children can jump in and help me deliver the rowboats."

She stepped into her boat and started the motor. In a few moments she was idling it alongside the ferry. "Jump!" she called.

One by one, Nan, Bert, then Charlie, leaped across the gap of water into the motorboat. Returning to the dock, they untied one of the smaller boats. Then, as the children held onto the rope, Aunt Sue drove the motorboat to a neighbor's dock to return the "borrowed" property to its owner. The operation was repeated until all the boats were returned.

While they were gone, Mr. Wiggins brought the ferryboat to the dock. Flossie and Freddie put down the gangplank and went ashore with Waggo.

As the little dog frisked about, Freddie was thinking about the mischievous people who had played the trick on them. Maybe he could find them!

"Waggo," he said, "you and I have a job to do. Make believe you're a bloodhound. We'll track down whoever tied these boats up."

Although Waggo was a fox terrier and did not know how to track scents as well as a bloodhound, he perked up his ears. The playful pet was always eager to join in any kind of game his young master suggested.

"Sniff the ground," Freddie ordered, pointing, "and lead me to the villains!"

Waggo put his nose down, at the same time beating the air happily with his tail. He scampered this way and that, then led Freddie from the dock toward the shore road.

"Keep after them!" Freddie encouraged Waggo.

The little boy, pretending he was an old-time sheriff, stuck out his chest. He felt very important as he followed Waggo along the street.

Halfway up the block the terrier saw a cat sitting on a white fence. Barking, he startled the animal, who leaped to the ground with Waggo in pursuit. The dog chased her up a tree. Then he noticed two young squirrels on the ground near by and went pell-mell after them through a newly planted garden.

"Come back, Waggo, come back. You're supposed to be trailing a villain!" shouted Freddie.

But serious business was not in Waggo's mind

at the moment. The dog returned to Freddie, picking up a twig on the way which he dropped at his master's feet.

"We can't play a game with this right now," Freddie scolded, and looked around to get his bearings.

The zigzag trail over which Waggo had led Freddie went past the very row of garages where Bert and Charlie had been thrown off their bicycles the day before. Just then, Freddie heard muffled laughter.

"Sh-h, Waggo, somebody's in one of these garages," the little boy whispered as he tiptoed toward one of the closed doors.

The closer Freddie got, the louder the laughter became. The double doors were open a few inches. Freddie held on to Waggo's collar and peeked in. The dog, too, nosed up and poked his head through.

Inside the garage were Danny and Jack, laughing as if over a big joke. They were only half turned toward the door and did not see Freddie and his dog.

Danny said, "Now they'll have to take the ferryboat all the way back!"

"And they'll think the dock is rented!" said Jack, laughing so hard he had to hold his sides. "That's one of the best jokes we ever played on the Bobbseys."

"Except for yesterday when we made Bert and Charlie fall off their bikes!" Danny said with a smirk. "Wowee, they sure took a super tumble!"

Freddie was furious. His first thought was to run to the dock and tell the others. But he also wanted to see what Danny and Jack were doing. Maybe they were planning another trick!

Freddie noticed that the boys had set up a wooden box in the center of the empty garage. On either side of the box they had placed two smaller ones as chairs. A package tied with a loose string lay on the table.

Glancing at his watch, Danny remarked, "Well, it's about time for lunch."

"After we eat," said Jack, "let's go down to the dock and watch the ferryboat come in. Boy, are the Bobbseys going to have a surprise!"

As he reached for the package, Waggo suddenly pushed through the open door, jumped up on the wooden box, and grabbed the package.

"Hey, scat, you mutt! I mean, come back!" Danny shouted as Waggo leaped from corner to corner, shaking the package vigorously.

"Oh, our ham sandwiches and cake!" moaned Jack, running after him. "Come back here with our lunch!"

But Waggo had no intention of dropping the package without first engaging in some frisky play. As the boys chased him out of the garage, Freddie howled with laughter.

"You're here!" Danny cried. "How did *you* get here?"

Freddie did not wait to answer. He ran as fast as his chubby legs would take him toward the dock, but when the older boys were not looking, hid in another garage and watched the fun.

Jack, meanwhile, had chased the dog up the alley and back again. Waggo had the string in his teeth and stopped now and then to shake the lunch vigorously. Finally a ham sandwich fell out and Waggo swallowed the meat.

"Hey, stop!" Jack shouted.

Waggo grabbed the package again. Out fell another sandwich, followed by a pickle and a few olives. Then a piece of cocoanut cake spattered to the ground.

"Ow!" Danny howled as Waggo ate more meat. "It's ruined!"

Waggo shook the now empty paper. Then he dropped it at Danny's feet and raced off toward the dock.

"I'll fix that dog and the whole Bobbsey family!" Jack threatened, purple with rage.

"And I'll punch Freddie especially for this," Danny shouted.

But Freddie was out of sight. When he reached the dock, the little boy told the story of the ruined lunch. Everyone laughed uproariously.

"It serves those boys right," Nan said, "for what they did to Bert and Charlie."

"And pretty nearly makes us square for putting those rowboats in our way." Bert chuckled. "Thanks, Freddie."

By this time a crowd of youngsters had gath-

ered to watch the ferryboat. The Bobbseys forgot about Danny and Jack and began telling the
boys and girls about the island project. All of
them were eager to make the trip to Mr. Wiggins' island.

"When will they start?" asked a red-haired
boy.

"As soon as we get the boat cleaned up and
painted," Bert replied.

"And carry things over to the island," Nan
added.

The Bobbseys spent the afternoon making
plans and starting their clean-up job. Tara came
over for a while to help the twins. About five
o'clock Aunt Sue came to tell them that she had
just phoned Mrs. Bobbsey, asking if the children
might have supper with her and Mr. Smith.

"This will be keen," Charlie said. "Aunt Sue's
a swell cook."

"And I want you to join us, too, Mr. Wiggins," Aunt Sue said.

They all thanked her and accepted. As they
started to leave the boat, Bert said suddenly,
"With Danny and Jack around we shouldn't
leave the boat unguarded. Mrs. Smith, would
you mind if we take turns eating?"

"I have another solution," Aunt Sue said,
smiling. "The man next door has a big police
dog named Prince. Maybe Mr. Brown will lend

him as a guard for your ferryboat. Suppose you boys run next door and find out."

When they made their request of Mr. Brown, he said certainly, Prince could guard the ferryboat. "I'll chain him at the dock right away," he offered.

In a few minutes the big dog lay down near the boat to keep curious onlookers at a safe distance. The boys went in to supper.

The Bobbseys, Charlie, and Mr. Wiggins enjoyed the delicious meal of roast lamb, peas, and mashed potatoes. As Aunt Sue was about to serve the dessert, which was angelfood cake, Prince set up a terrific barking.

Bert jumped up from the table. "Something's wrong!" he cried.

CHAPTER X

A SLIPPERY ZEBRA

PRINCE continued to bark as everyone rushed to look outside. Bert was the first to the door. "A man is running away from the dock!" he exclaimed.

All the children caught a glimpse of the fugitive as he disappeared down the street.

"He's the one who tried to buy Tara's headdress at the school fair!" Flossie cried out.

"Are you sure?" Nan asked.

Flossie was certain that he was the same person—the man who had been with the blond woman in Tara's fortunetelling booth. "Remember, he was real mean to Tara 'cause she wouldn't sell him her headdress," Flossie reminded the others.

"What was he doing here?" Charlie wondered. "Do you think he wanted to steal your ferryboat?"

"He can't do that!" Freddie cried. "It's ours!"

"Indeed he can't," Mr. Wiggins said, smiling. "Now don't you worry, little man."

All of them tried in vain to get the man out of their minds.

"Anyway," said Nan as they returned to eat their dessert, "Prince is certainly a good watchdog. I guess we shan't have to worry with him around."

When they finished eating, the children and Mr. Wiggins thanked Aunt Sue for her hospitality. A few minutes later Mrs. Bobbsey drove up and took them home.

The twins and their friends were up early the next morning. There was much to be done! Nan telephoned Charlie Mason, then Nellie Parks, putting them in charge of obtaining the swings, slides, and other equipment for the island playground.

"But how are we going to carry everything out there if you keep the ferryboat docked to paint?" Nellie asked.

Nan told her she had arranged everything with her father. Mr. Bobbsey had a motor barge at the lumberyard which was operated by Captain Chester, called Cap for short. He would help load the equipment onto the barge and take it to the island.

"Cap will cement the swings into the ground,"

Nan told her friend. "All you and Charlie have to do is find the toys, Nellie."

Meanwhile Freddie and Bert accompanied Mr. Wiggins to a hardware store to buy a supply of brushes and paint for the little ferryboat.

"What color do you want to paint it?" the clerk asked after Bert had purchased some large brushes.

"Red," the boy decided. "And tan decks." The cabin and pilot house would also be red. In order to save time, the clerk said he would deliver the material to Aunt Sue Smith's dock.

When the two boys arrived home, they found Nan and Flossie excitedly waiting for them. "Guess what, Bert!" Nan cried out. "We're going to have a merry-go-round for the island."

"Swell! Where did you get it?"

Nan said Nellie had just telephoned the good news. She had found a small, hand-operated merry-go-round at a used-toy shop. The dealer had agreed to let the Bobbseys rent it for their island project.

"Nellie's mother is driving over to pick it up in their station wagon," Nan continued. "She'll take it direct to Dad's lumberyard."

Shortly afterwards Charlie phoned Bert, saying he had located a set of old schoolyard swings and two used slides at the Board of Education storehouse.

"Mr. Tetlow has ordered them sent to your dad's lumberyard," Charlie reported happily.

"Boy, that's great!" Bert said and told his brother and sisters.

The twins were so excited, they could hardly settle down long enough to eat their lunch.

"Our island playground will be bee-yoo-ti-ful," Flossie cooed as she sipped her chocolate milk through a straw.

"My goodness!" Dinah said. "I think you-all are too wound up to eat the apple pies I made."

"Not me!" Bert protested. "Watch me unwind!"

"Same here!" Freddie agreed.

"And I'd like to try it too," said Mr. Wiggins, who by now was thoroughly enjoying family life at the Bobbsey home.

After lunch the children's father drove them all to the lumberyard. The equipment for the island playground stood on a large dock. Alongside the dock a small barge was tied up.

"Oh, look at the neat swings!" cried Freddie.

"And there's Tara's tent," said Nan.

As the children piled out of the car and ran toward the water, a short, smiling man came from the cabin of the barge.

"Hi, Cap!" Bert greeted him.

Cap Chester had once been a sea captain and still had what Mr. Bobbsey called "sea legs." He ambled toward them with a grin and tilted his captain's cap back on his head.

"Hello, young'uns," he said. "Well, I'm glad to see you're wearing dungarees today. You can help me load this stuff onto the barge."

"That's what we're here for," said Bert.

Nan introduced Cap to Mr. Wiggins, then everybody set about to load the swings, slides, and merry-go-round onto the barge. Mr. Bobbsey remained to lend a hand, for some of the pipes were very heavy. By pulling and tugging, Bert, Charlie, and Mr. Wiggins moved the small merry-go-round across the gangplank.

"Whew!" said Mr. Wiggins, mopping his brow. "Where do you think we ought to put this, Mr. Bobbsey?" he called.

"Move it toward the center of the barge."

"Okay, let's go!"

As the men and the boys pushed the merry-go-round across the deck, Flossie ran up to them. "Please, I want a ride," she said.

Without waiting for permission, Flossie climbed up onto the back of a wooden zebra and bounced up and down several times. "Ooo, he's slippery!" the little girl cried out.

"Easy there," Bert warned. "You might throw this off balance before it's tied down."

As he said this, Flossie leaned to one side and waved to Nan.

"Hey, look out!" Charlie warned.

The merry-go-round suddenly tilted and, had it not been for the combined strength of Mr. Wiggins and the boys, it might have fallen into the water!

As it was, Flossie tumbled off and rolled toward the water. "Help!" she cried. Nan made a lunge for the little girl and caught her just in time.

"That's a bucking bronco, not a zebra!" Freddie said, bursting into laughter.

The merry-go-round was pushed to its proper place on the deck. Then the other equipment was stowed on the barge. When everything was ready Mr. Bobbsey called to Sam, who had been loading lumber onto one of the trucks.

"Suppose you and Cap take these things to the island and set them up," he said.

"Yes, sir!" Sam replied.

For once the twins did not beg to go. They had work of their own to do on the ferryboat. Mrs. Bobbsey drove down for them in the station wagon and took them out to the Smiths. Aunt Sue came out to greet them and said that the paint and brushes had been delivered and were on the boat.

Freddie inquired whether any more prowlers had been around and was told that the night had passed quietly. "Prince is a good watchman," said Aunt Sue, "even when he's asleep!"

The children petted the dog, then took him back to his home until they should need him again.

Soon the Bobbseys were busy shaking up the cans of paint in preparation for brightening the ferryboat. When the paints were thoroughly mixed, Mr. Wiggins suggested that they start with the pilot house and work down. The taller group would do the upper three quarters, Freddie and Flossie the lower part. The sides of the boat would be painted next and finally the decks.

The twins painted as neatly and quickly as Mrs. Bobbsey and Mr. Wiggins.

Freddie was the only one who got any paint on himself. As they were working on the pilot house, he got a streak across his forehead and one spot on his chin. Mrs. Bobbsey wiped them off, saying he was doing very well.

She had no sooner made the remark than over went the little boy's can of paint! Fortunately, it was the tan color and was quickly spread on the deck by all the painters.

When the pilot house was finished Nan stood back admiringly. "The ferry's going to look lovely!" she said.

"Just bee-yoo-ti-ful!" Flossie sighed.

"But now comes the hard part," Bert said. "Painting the sides of our ferryboat."

Freddie and Flossie were not allowed to do this, so they sat on Aunt Sue's lawn to watch. The older twins were careful as they leaned over the side of the boat. It was hard work and they, as well as their mother and Mr. Wiggins, had to pause many times to rest their arms and backs. After reaching down as far as they could, there was still an unpainted section just above the water line.

"We'll have to do it from a rowboat," Bert remarked, and they asked Aunt Sue if they might use hers.

"Of course you may," she told them. "There's an anchor in the front of the boat which will hold you steady."

Bert and Nan climbed into Aunt Sue's boat and rowed to the far side of the ferry. After this was painted they circled around to work on the other side and the ends.

When they finished, everyone stood off to admire the ferryboat. How beautiful it looked! The red sides and the cabin and pilot house sparkled in the slanting rays of the sun.

Meanwhile, Freddie and Flossie went to get Prince and chained him on the dock. "Don't you go near the ferryboat and rub paint on yourself," Flossie warned him.

"It's five o'clock and time to go home," Mrs. Bobbsey said finally as the children cleaned their paintbrushes and put the tops back on the cans.

When they had washed in the Smiths' house they said good-by to Aunt Sue and started home, dropping Mr. Wiggins at a friend's house on the way.

"Oh, my goodness!" Mrs. Bobbsey exclaimed as they neared their house. "I left my purse on the Smiths' dock. We'll have to go back."

When they reached the dock Mrs. Bobbsey

suggested that Bert run over for the purse while she drove up the street a short distance and turned around. He jumped out of the car and hurried over to where his mother's purse lay near the ferryboat.

"I wonder where Prince is," Bert thought. "I guess he must have been taken home for his supper," he decided.

By the time he had picked up the purse Mrs. Bobbsey was on her way back. Suddenly she stopped the car. Bert could hear those in it cry out in dismay.

"Bert, come here!" Nan shouted.

"Isn't it awful!" Flossie wailed.

"Who did it?" Freddie called angrily.

Bert hastened to see what they were looking at. Seeing it, he groaned.

Someone had painted ugly, zigzag black stripes on one side of their ferryboat!

CHAPTER XI

THE FISHING-POLE CLUE

"OUR paint job is ruined!" Nan cried, hurrying from the car with the others.

By standing on Mr. Brown's lawn, the Bobbseys could get a good view of the zigzag smears of black paint across the side of the red ferryboat.

Tears came to Flossie's eyes. "Whoever did it was the meanest old meanie!" she sobbed, stamping her foot.

Hearing the children's cries, Mrs. Brown ran outside.

"Oh dear!" she exclaimed. She said Prince had watched the ferryboat faithfully, but that Mr. Brown had taken him inside half an hour before to give the dog his supper.

"That's probably when the vandals did their mischief," Mrs. Bobbsey suggested.

"They must have sneaked up in a rowboat,"

Bert guessed. Measuring the height of the zig-zag lines with his eye, he added, "It must have been done by a very tall fellow, because the black lines reach nearly as high as the deck."

Nan thought it must have taken two people to make the lines. "And I'll bet they probably tied paint brushes onto poles to reach way up to the deck."

"I see it!" Freddie cried out, pointing to the beach. Lying on the pebbly shore was a long bamboo pole. "Maybe it's somebody's fishing rod."

The little boy ran over to get it. When he brought back the long bamboo fishing pole, the Bobbseys knew they had a real clue. On one end of the rod was some black paint!

"Nan, you were right," Bert said admiringly.

Suddenly Nan announced that this had given her another idea. She would tie one of their own brushes to the pole, get into Aunt Sue's rowboat, and daub red paint over the black lines.

"Good," Bert said, "and while you're doing that, Freddie and I will look around for the sneaks who did this."

The boys hurried off. Nan got a brush and a can of red paint from Aunt Sue Smith's cellar, then rigged up her long-handled paint brush. Putting them all into the rowboat, she rowed to the side of the ferry.

After dropping anchor, she started to paint over the black lines. This was hard to do because each time she needed more paint on the brush, Nan had to turn the pole upside down. The paint dripped and splashed, but Nan managed to keep it out of the rowboat. Finally Nan covered most of the zigzag lines.

"That's pretty!" Flossie called to her, leaning over the railing of the ferryboat. "But there's one place you missed," she added.

Flossie pointed to a black line near the deck and offered to reach down and paint it. Nan, however, thought that she could manage it with the pole. Balancing herself on the center seat of the rowboat, Nan stood on tiptoe to paint the spot.

"Careful!" Flossie warned, as the little boat tilted slightly.

"Don't worry, honey, I'll get it!" Nan said, daubing red paint over the black.

Finally she had it all covered except one small square. Nan held the long pole in the fingers of her right hand and stretched as far as she could.

"There—I—have—it!" she muttered. But before she could lower the pole into the boat, Nan teetered, leaning far over the water.

"Ooo-eee, look out!" Flossie cried fearfully.

Her sister dropped the pole and clawed the air as she tried to regain her balance. But she had leaned too far. The boat tipped. With a little scream, Nan fell into the lake!

After her went the can of red paint. When Nan bobbed to the surface, her hair and face were covered with red paint.

"Oh, Nan!" Flossie wailed and called loudly for her mother to come.

Mrs. Bobbsey and Aunt Sue rushed over. They reached the shore just as Nan walked out of the water.

"Oh, my goodness!" Mrs. Bobbsey said.

Flossie, over her fright, began to giggle. "Nan looks like a painted Indian," she said.

Aunt Sue ran for a Turkish towel and some soap she used for removing paint. Nan was given a shampoo in the lake.

In the meantime Mr. Smith put on his bathing trunks and swam out to retrieve the boat.

After Nan's hair had had several rinsings, she went into the house to take off her wet things. Aunt Sue provided her with dry clothing.

When Nan came out of the house, Flossie said, "Wait till Bert and Freddie hear what happened to you!"

During this time the two boys had been busy on their search of the culprits who had streaked paint on the ferryboat.

"I have an idea it was Danny and Jack," Bert said. "They might be using that garage as a hideout. Can you lead me to it, Freddie?"

"Sure, it's right over this way."

He retraced his steps over the trail he had taken with Waggo. Bert recognized the alley in which he and Charlie had been thrown from their bicycles.

Soon the brothers were at the garage where Waggo had snatched up Danny and Jack's lunch. The two boys began walking on tiptoe.

"I hear someone," Bert whispered as they approached the half-open door.

Looking inside, they saw Danny and Jack. The two pals were kneeling on a newspaper spread on the garage floor. An open can of turpentine was resting on the paper. They were very carefully wiping their hands with rags dipped in the turpentine.

Bert stepped through the doorway with Freddie following. He gave Freddie a wink, cleared his throat noisily, and said, "Hi there, fellows! Want a little help with that paint remover?"

Seeing them, Jack and Danny were so surprised, they could hardly speak for a moment. First one, then the other, sprang to his feet. Danny was the first to find his voice.

"What are you doing here?" he asked hoarsely. "I'm getting fed up with you Bobbseys always sneaking up on us."

"Yeah!" Jack agreed angrily, trying to hide his hands behind his back. "Scram!"

Before Danny had a chance to hide his own

hands, Bert noticed that they were covered with black paint. Now he was sure the boys had done the damage to the ferryboat. It was another attempt to stall the Bobbseys' project.

Though Bert was still angry over the zigzag lines painted on the ferry, he was amused at the bullies' guilty embarrassment. "I thought you fellows wouldn't mind doing me a favor," he said, smiling.

Danny merely grunted and Bert continued, "I thought you'd like to help us find a clue."

"A clue to what?" Jack demanded.

"To the boys who messed up the paint job on our ferryboat," Freddie piped up.

"We don't go snooping," Danny said, glaring. "Besides, you're the last people I'd ever help!"

Bert tried to hold his temper. "Well, you wanted to help us find a dock for our ferryboat," he said. "You must have snooped around or you wouldn't have known we had it."

"Why, we overheard Sam Johnson telling about the boat to a friend of his in the fish market," Jack hurried to say. Then he gasped, as he realized he had been led into a trap.

"Get out of here!" Danny demanded.

"Not until you tell me how you got that black paint on your hands," retorted Bert.

"You think you're smart," Danny sneered. "Well, I'll tell you. We were painting a chair."

He pointed to a dim corner of the garage, where an old kitchen chair stood, half covered with black paint.

"That suit you?" Jack asked.

The brothers glanced about for another possible clue. Suddenly Freddie spied a long bamboo pole standing in one corner of the garage. It was exactly like the one they had found on the beach near Aunt Sue's cottage. He nudged Bert and pointed. Bert dashed over to look at it.

One end of the fishing rod was covered with black paint!

"You *were* the ones who messed up our boat!" Bert Bobbsey said angrily.

"Now look here!" Danny Rugg said, flustered by the accusation.

"Explain this!" Bert demanded, holding up the pole.

CHAPTER XII

A TWIN CONTEST

DANNY and Jack were angry at Bert's charge. "I'll hit you for that!" Danny shouted.

"Me, too!" said Jack, and the boys dashed forward with fists raised.

Knowing that he could not tackle both of them at once, even with Freddie's help, Bert tried something else. He held the pole across his chest with both hands. Shoving it toward the onrushing boys, he stopped them short. They went sprawling onto the garage floor.

Jack Westley had the fight knocked out of him and was content to rub a bruised leg. But Danny sprang to his feet and pitched into Bert. Fists flew for a few moments with neither boy gaining the advantage.

But finally Bert saw his chance and landed a punch on Danny's chin. The boy howled in pain and rubbed his jaw. He was just about to fling a punch at Bert when the garage door opened wide.

"What's going on here?" said a tall man. "Jack, explain this!"

The newcomer was Mr. Westley, Jack's father, who had driven up to put his car in the garage.

"These Bobbseys came here to pick on us," Jack whimpered.

"We did not!" Freddie spoke up quickly, and blurted out the story of the black paint.

Mr. Westley turned to his son and Danny. "Did you boys smear the ferryboat?" he asked.

Jack hung his head. Even though he was a mischief-maker, he would not tell his father a lie. "It wasn't my idea, Dad."

"Yes, it was!" Danny cried out, turning on his friend. Then he added, "But we were only having fun. Besides the Bobbseys' dog ate our lunch."

Jack's father frowned. "It seems to me that you fellows ought to get along better," he said. "What started all this rumpus, anyway?"

Upon further questioning, Mr. Westley drew an admission from his son and Danny that they had caused the bicycle accident of Bert and Charlie. It was they, too, who had tied up all the rowboats at Aunt Sue's docks so that the ferryboat could not land.

"Well," Mr. Westley said sternly, "you'd better stop playing pranks, or someone may get hurt."

When he finished speaking, Danny sulked out of the garage and hurried off. Freddie and Bert made their way back to the dock where the ferryboat was tied up.

Seeing Nan in strange clothes, they asked what had happened and laughed to hear how she had fallen into the water. Then Bert told of the boys' adventure.

"Well, I hope they won't bother you any more," Mrs. Bobbsey said. "And now we really must go home."

Before leaving, Bert and Freddie looked at the ferryboat and praised Nan for her paint job. How nice it looked! Prince was put on guard, this time on the boat itself.

When the twins arrived home they found Dinah and Sam in the kitchen. The children immediately plied Sam with questions about his day on the island.

"We made out fine," he reported with a wide grin. He told the children that the swings had been cemented into place. The slides and the merry-go-round, too, were ready for visitors.

"It sure enough looks like an amusement park," Sam declared. "Boy, we have everything over there now except a fortuneteller." He gave Dinah a big wink.

As he said this the jolly woman cried out, "My goodness, old Dinah's memory must be failing. Nan, there was a phone call for you while you were away."

"Who was it?" Nan asked.

"Tara, and she has something mighty important to tell you."

Nan hurried to the telephone. Bert went upstairs, leaving the younger twins talking to Sam and Dinah. Now, for the first time, they saw that a pile of newspaper clippings lay on the table. In each was a picture of a child with a number underneath it.

"Are you and Dinah playing games?" Freddie asked Sam.

"This is Dinah's game," Sam replied, looking solemnly at his wife. "Dinah thinks she's sure enough going to win a contest."

"What kind of a contest?" Flossie asked eagerly.

"It's a twin contest, honey child," Dinah replied, sorting through the pile of pictures.

She went on to explain that each week several photographs of unmatched twins appeared in the newspaper. Then the following week more would be printed. The idea was to match them all properly by the end of the contest.

"I'm sure an expert on twins," Dinah said, "so maybe I have a chance to win this contest."

When Freddie inquired what the prize was, Sam eagerly replied that it was a trip to Washington, D. C.

"And whoever wins can take a friend along," Sam added with a big grin. "You'll take me with you, won't you, Dinah?"

"Hush with that sugar talk!" Dinah replied, laughing. "I won't promise anything unless you take me to the movies tonight, Sam."

Freddie, recalling a joke Teddy Blake had told him, said, "Dinah's made a trip already."

Sam's eyes grew wide with amazement. "She has—already?" he asked.

"Sure. Dinah tripped over the kitchen broom," the little boy said, laughing.

"Oh my!" Sam chuckled. Dinah and Flossie giggled too.

At that moment Waggo and Snap whined at the kitchen door to come in, and Flossie opened it. Snap lay down at once, but Waggo began frisking about and presently jumped onto a chair by the table. Seeing the pictures, he put up his paws and sniffed at them.

"Scat, dog!" Dinah cried. "You're mussing up the contest!"

Suddenly Waggo playfully took one of the papers in his mouth, jumped down, and started to run off. Freddie and Flossie dashed after him.

"Drop that!" they cried.

But Waggo had no intention of doing this. He raced up the stairs, the twins after him.

"What'll we do?" Freddie said.

He and Flossie realized that even when they caught the dog he would not drop the picture. If they tried to take it out of his mouth, the paper would tear.

"I know a way," said Flossie.

She turned and ran downstairs. Going to the cooky jar, the little girl took out a fat sugar cooky and hurried back upstairs with it.

"I'll trade, Waggo," she said. "One cooky for one twin."

Waggo could not resist this. He dropped the picture, which Freddie quickly scooped up. The dog gobbled up the cooky, then they all went back to the kitchen.

When the twins handed over the clipping, Dinah was delighted. "Bless you!" she cried. "You've saved my trip for me!"

"I hope you win it," Flossie said, "and please take Sam to Washington if you go."

Sam's face broke into a gleaming smile. "Well, Dinah, if the twins want me to go to Washington, guess you'd better take me along," he told his wife. "Might be good luck in the contest if you promise."

Dinah could not help chuckling. "That's some figuring, Sam," she said. "But maybe you're right. So if I do win, we'll both take the trip."

Just then Nan came running into the kitchen. "Oh!" she exclaimed. "Such wonderful news! I can hardly wait to see them."

The others looked mystified and Dinah said, "Now, Nan, you just calm down and start from the beginning. I reckon you left out some of the story. Tell us who and where and when."

"I'm so excited." Nan had to pause to catch her breath and Freddie urged, "Hurry, Nan, what *is* it?"

"What do you think?" his older sister cried. "Tara's grandmother and uncle have just arrived from Spain. Isn't that marvelous?"

Freddie let out a whoop. "You mean the bull-fighter uncle?" As Nan nodded, he said, "Oh boy! Maybe he'll have his bullfighter's pants and hat and his special red cape that he uses to scare the bulls."

With these words the boy grabbed a dish towel and, waving it wildly, started prancing around. Everyone laughed and Dinah said, "Looks like we got a bullfighter right here in the kitchen!"

Flossie meanwhile had been standing still, her blue eyes wide. "Just think," she murmured, "a famous gypsy fortuneteller! Oh, I wish we could see her!"

"That's exactly what we're going to do," Nan told her. "Tara has invited us to dinner tomorrow night to meet them."

"Goody!" said Flossie, and Freddie shouted for joy. "Wait'll everybody hears we met a real live bullfighter!" he exclaimed.

Dinah and Sam had been taking in the news with keen interest. Now Dinah spoke up. "I reckon that fortuneteller sure could tell me about the twin contest!"

"Maybe," Sam agreed. "But you don't need your palm read for that. I have a feeling you'll get first prize anyhow."

As everyone listened intently, Nan went on to explain that the twins had been invited over to Tara's home for another reason. "We're going to see the gypsy fortuneteller's wonderful head-dress and hear the story about it."

"That's swell!" said Freddie. "I love stories about gypsies."

"And Tara has another surprise for us," Nan went on.

"What is it?" asked Bert, who had just walked in.

"Tara wouldn't tell me," Nan replied. "She said we'll have to wait until tomorrow to find out."

CHAPTER XIII

A MIDNIGHT PROWLER

ANOTHER surprise for the Bobbseys!

"We're the surprisingest family in Lakeport," said Flossie. "But I want to know what Tara's going to tell us."

"Maybe," Bert guessed, "Tara's mother is going to serve a special Spanish supper."

Freddie looked worried. "It will probably burn our mouths," he said, remembering a hot Mexican-Spanish dish he had once eaten.

Nan thought that Mrs. O'Toole might do a Spanish gypsy dance for them. The guessing went on until bedtime for the smaller twins. They always retired earlier than Bert and Nan.

Before Bert went to bed, he took Waggo and Snap for a long walk in the cool summer evening. As the dogs ran about, the boy found his footsteps leading to the lake shore. As usual, Waggo wanted to frolic near the water. He found a stick which he picked up and laid at the feet of the boy.

"So you want to play," Bert laughed, picking it up. "Okay, fetch!" The boy threw the stick along the beach where there were lights.

Both Waggo and Snap ran after it, but the younger dog got it. Bert threw the stick several times, with Waggo always the winner. Snap gave up in disgust.

Bert was about to return with the dogs when his attention was attracted to the winking of a light far out across the water.

"It must be on a boat," Bert thought as he watched it. But the light did not move. "That's out near Mr. Wiggins' island," the boy told himself.

Bert began to worry as the light remained stationary. "I'll bet that *is* on the island," he said half aloud.

His first thought was that Danny and Jack might be trying to damage the playground that had been set up. Then Bert wondered if the mysterious man they had seen was stealing the small merry-go-round or some of the other equipment.

"I must find out!"

Whistling for the dogs, Bert ran home as fast as he could with Snap and Waggo behind him. Breathless, he hurried into the living room where his father was reading a newspaper.

"My goodness," said Mr. Bobbsey, looking up, "are you practicing for the track team, Bert?"

"Dad, something's wrong!"

"What do you mean?"

"Someone's on the island," Bert stated. "Was anyone left on guard?"

"Not that I know of," Mr. Bobbsey replied, rising from his chair. "Why don't you ask Sam?"

The boy hurried to the third-floor rooms occupied by Sam and Dinah, and quickly asked the question.

"We didn't leave a soul on the island," Sam said. "And I know it isn't Mr. Wiggins, 'cause he's visiting a friend for the evening."

Sam accompanied the boy downstairs to the living room. Nan and Mrs. Bobbsey had come in after hearing Bert's excited voice.

"If somebody's over there we'd better go see what he's doing!" Bert cried.

Mrs. Bobbsey agreed that the intruder might steal or damage the equipment.

"And that would spoil our whole project," Nan said, worried. "Please may we go to the island right away, Mother?"

"You may if your father goes with you," she replied.

"All right," Mr. Bobbsey told Nan, "you and Bert and I. And Sam, you come too."

"How are we going to get there?" Bert asked.

This was a problem indeed. The ferryboat was very slow, and going by rowboat was out of the question.

"Maybe we can borrow Aunt Sue Smith's motorboat," Nan suggested.

"Good idea," her father said.

Nan hurried to the phone and in a few minutes had Aunt Sue Smith's permission to use the fast boat. Taking flashlights, Bert and Nan followed their father and Sam to the station wagon.

When they arrived at the Smiths' Aunt Sue had the boat in readiness with the outboard motor running and oars in the bottom in case the engine went dead.

"If there's a prowler on the island I certainly hope you catch him," she said as the four stepped into the boat and she climbed out.

Nan sat in front while Mr. Bobbsey and Sam took the middle seats. Bert operated the motor and the tiller, having driven motorboats many times around Lake Metoka.

"Shove off!" he called to his sister and Nan pushed the prow away from the dock. Bert kept it in a steady line toward the island where the flickering light could still be seen. Everyone hoped the intruder would not take the equipment and leave before they could get there.

As they neared the island, Mr. Bobbsey suggested that Bert turn off the running lights and cut the motor so as not to warn the prowler of their approach. He and Sam would man the oars and come up silently to the shore.

The light was still there, and Bert whispered excitedly, "We'll catch him easily!"

The four in the boat made plans. The two men would jump off first and as they did, Nan, in the prow, would beam her flash on the intruder.

"Get ready!" Mr. Bobbsey said tensely.

The moment the bow touched the beach he and Sam hopped quietly ashore. At the same instant Nan flashed her light.

"There he is, Dad!" Bert cried out as the beam fell upon a shadowy figure. The prowler quickly extinguished his own light and dashed off among the trees back of the beach.

"Halt!" cried Mr. Bobbsey. "We won't harm you! We just want to know what you're doing here."

But the fellow did not stop. "Get him!" Bert shouted as he and his sister jumped ashore.

They pulled the boat up on the beach, then caught up to Mr. Bobbsey and Sam, who were already racing after the fugitive. Up ahead they could still see the dim figure scurrying toward the opposite shore.

"Look, Dad, he's running across the beach!" Nan said as they reached the end of the woods.

"There he is, Dad!" Bert cried

With a burst of speed the intruder gave a yell and dashed to the water's edge. At the same time a motorboat offshore started up.

"He's going to escape!" Bert yelled.

The man splashed through the water and in a few moments had taken off in the boat.

The disappointed group stood silent a moment, then Bert suggested going after him and his companion with their boat.

Mr. Bobbsey shook his head. "By the time we could get back to it, the fellow would have too much of a head start. Anyway, he may not have harmed the equipment."

"Let's look!" Bert urged.

As they hurried back to the other side of the island, Sam pointed out the location of the playground that he and Cap had set up. Breathless from excitement and the chase, they came upon the site. It was a level spot of sandy ground near the shore and was fringed by little clumps of birch trees.

"This is keen!" Bert told Sam, who had selected the location.

"It's near the ferryboat dock, too," Nan put in, "so our visitors won't have far to walk once they arrive here."

As they came closer, the twins saw, to their relief, that nothing appeared to be disturbed. The equipment was laid out on the sides of an imaginary square, with the swings along one side, the slides on another, and the little merry-go-round on the third.

Bert quickly examined the seats of the swings. They were intact, as were the chains which connected them to the top bar.

Nan found that the slides were smooth and had not been tampered with. Finally, the carousel responded easily to the hand wheel which sent it whirling. Delighted and relieved that everything was safe, Bert and Nan hopped up on a horse and a tiger and spun around several times.

"What's that?" Nan asked, glancing toward a low, boxlike structure hardly visible in the moonlight.

The twins hopped off the carousel and ran over to it.

"A big sandbox!" Nan exclaimed. "Where did it come from?"

"I made it for you all," Sam said proudly. "It was going to be a surprise."

"That's great!" Bert said, patting Sam on the back. "Now even the smallest kids can have fun here."

Nan added, "Now that everything is all right, we can go ahead with our plans for the money-making project. But the prowler was here for some reason," she declared. Nan beamed her light here and there, but did not pick up any clues.

Bert had an idea. "Let's retrace our steps to the place where we surprised that man. Maybe we'll find something there."

They hurried to the place and once more criss-crossed the ground with their flashlights.

"Someone was digging here," Nan called out excitedly, pointing to a spot where the ground had been turned over at the edge of the beach. "And recently, too!"

A moment later, Bert discovered a long-handled shovel. Using it, he dug into the dirt but could find nothing.

"Maybe that man was just diggin' for fishin' worms," Sam suggested.

But Mr. Bobbsey and the twins were not satisfied with this explanation. They began to search farther. Just then the moon, which had been hiding behind low, overhanging clouds, burst forth into a clear patch of sky. It was almost as bright as day on the island.

"Now we can see better!" Nan said and the twins cast their eyes over the ground near by.

Seeing several strange-looking, grassy hollows, Nan said to Bert, "What do you suppose made those little sunken spots?"

The twins dashed over to them and dropped to their knees to look more closely.

"The grass was taken off and then laid back in place," said Bert, reaching his fingers under a piece of loose turf.

As he lifted up a piece of the loose grass, they could see that the earth under it was loose as if it had been shoveled out, then put in again recently. Excitedly Nan began to dig with the shovel. Suddenly she cried out:

"Bert, I've found something!"

CHAPTER XIV

TELLTALE FOOTPRINTS

SAM and Mr. Bobbsey hurried to Nan's side as she thrust her hand deep into the hole and pulled out a leather sack.

"Land sakes," Sam chuckled, "this is like findin' a pirate's treasure."

"Hurry, sis, let's see what's in it!" Bert urged his twin.

The girl loosened the leather drawstring and opened the mouth of the sack. A second later she gasped, "It's money!"

She held up a roll of bills which Bert quickly counted. The ones, fives, and tens totaled exactly two hundred dollars.

"Wow!" Bert exclaimed. "Do you suppose it's hidden loot?"

"It may be," said his father. "In any case this looks like a job for the police."

"We ought to call them right away," said Bert.

But since there was no phone on the island, it meant leaving at once.

"I think we should stay and search some more," Bert spoke up.

Nan agreed. "That man might come back if we all leave."

Sam smiled. "Mr. Bobbsey," he said, "you all are better detectives than I am. Let me take the boat and call the police."

"All right, Sam."

Sam hurried to the beach, got into the motorboat, and soon was humming back across the
lake.

Meanwhile, Bert, Nan, and Mr. Bobbsey
searched the island, using their flashlights, but
found no more spots that had been dug up, nor
any new clues.

By the time they had recrossed the island
twice, the twins heard the sound of a motorboat
and ran to the shore. It was Sam returning. He
told them he had gone to Aunt Sue Smith's home
to telephone the police.

"They promised to come here at once," Sam
said. "Listen, I think I hear their launch now."

In the distance could be heard the roar of a
powerful motor. At the same time a big searchlight stabbed a yellow beam across the water.

"Here they come!" Bert cried out.

A few minutes later the police launch pulled
alongside the old ferryboat dock, and four officers stepped ashore, carrying two powerful
searchlights.

Mr. Bobbsey and the twins quickly told their
story, and Nan turned over the sack of money to
Lieutenant Pyle, who was in charge. Thanking
her, he removed the bills and turned the sack
inside out, but there was no writing on it to reveal the identity of the owner.

"I'm glad you found this," the lieutenant said.

"It *may* be the property of some innocent person, but I think more likely it will turn out to be stolen money. We'll take a look around."

The searchlight from the launch made the area almost as bright as daylight. The police also carried powerful hand flashlights.

"These lights of yours sure are bright," Bert said, as he walked alongside the officers in a new search of the island.

First they went to the place where Nan had found the sack. Using small shovels from the launch, the police dug hole after hole but uncovered no other treasure. After that, they turned their attention to the path which the fugitive had taken in his dash across the island.

"Keep a good lookout," Lieutenant Pyle said. "Any little clue may help us."

Walking along slowly, the four police, the Bobbseys, and Sam Johnson spread out in a long line, combing every bit of ground as they went.

Suddenly there was a rustling in a patch of underbrush. "Maybe someone's hiding in there," Sam whispered. "Listen!"

Bert and Nan tingled with excitement as the lieutenant ordered, "Surround him, men!"

The police approached the brush cautiously, their powered lights probing ahead.

"Whoever you are, come out of there with your hands up!" Lieutenant Pyle called out.

"And no funny business," another policeman said.

The twins' hearts thumped as they watched, wide-eyed. Was another prowler lurking in the brush—was he about to be flushed from his hiding place?

The policemen closed in farther, their lights stabbing the brush. Suddenly from under one of the bushes jumped a big white-and-brown jack rabbit. It bounded away.

Everyone laughed and Lieutenant Pyle said, "Well, it took eight of us to find that four-legged boy!"

"Yes," said Sam. Then, shaking his head, he murmured, "We sure enough missed a good rabbit stew!"

As the group worked its way across the island, Bert, in the lead with the head officer, nearly stepped on a small piece of white paper. Bending over to pick it up, he said, "This might be a clue, Lieutenant."

"What is it?"

"Looks like a corner of an envelope," Bert replied as he turned the white paper over in his hands. "Say! There's a number on it."

As the man flashed his light directly onto the paper, Bert could clearly make out the number "24" typed near the edge of it.

"Maybe it's part of an address," Nan said.

"I think you're right," the lieutenant said. Taking a notebook from his pocket, he wrote down the time and place where the paper had been found.

The searchers continued on, finally reaching the beach from which the stranger had escaped.

"Careful now," the lieutenant warned everybody. "Approach slowly so we don't ruin his footprints."

"Here's one," Bert called out immediately.

"And I see one too," Sam added.

The policeman rushed to where the two stood together.

"Good!" Lieutenant Pyle said, bending over to examine the prints. They were close to the water's edge where the sand was soft.

The prints of a left and a right shoe were clearly pressed into the soft earth. The policemen immediately went to work measuring the prints. One of the officers pulled a small camera from his pocket and took a flash bulb picture of them. It was developed immediately inside the camera and a minute later the picture was ready. Everyone crowded around to see it.

"How interesting!" Nan exclaimed, examining the prints. Then she added, "See the lion's head?"

"Where?" the lieutenant asked.

Another policeman pulled a magnifying glass

from his pocket and carefully studied the picture.

"You're right, miss. The prowler wore Lion's Head brand rubber heels on his shoes."

The police were happy, they said, to have this clue and said with luck it might lead them to the prowler. The sackful of money especially interested Lieutenant Pyle.

"You Bobbseys may have stumbled onto the hiding place of thieves," he said.

The officer explained that several small business firms in Lakeport had been robbed recently. A number of suspects had been picked up, but all had been freed and the real thieves had not been caught.

Mr. Bobbsey remarked that a lonely island like this one would make an ideal spot where thieves might hide money or jewelry. "Evidently they took away all but the one bag," he said.

"Either that or they plan to bring more and bury the loot in those other holes they dug," the lieutenant suggested.

Bert wanted to know whether the thieves would return to a place from which they had been chased away.

"They might," the officer answered. "Anyway, we'll post a guard on the island in case the thief or thieves do come back."

"That will be protection for the children's

playground project too," said Mr. Bobbsey.

"We'll be glad to guard that too," the lieutenant said.

One of the policemen was posted immediately
and the other three, after thanking the Bobbseys
and Sam for their information, and giving them
a receipt for the money they had found, started
back to Lakeport.

"I think we'd better go home, too," Mr. Bobbsey said. "It's nearly midnight."

It had been such an exciting evening that
neither Bert nor Nan realized how tired they
were. Now their eyelids began to feel heavy as
they climbed into the motorboat.

But, like a true detective, Bert refused to take
a nap on the return trip. Instead he took the
tiller again. Soon they were back at Aunt Sue's
dock, and the men tied up the boat. They all
spoke to Prince, then walked quietly toward
Mr. Bobbsey's car. The Smiths, hearing them,
came to the door and called to them.

"Everything's okay," Nan said. "The police
came. They think the money may have been
stolen. A man's on guard at the island now."

The Bobbseys and Sam drove home. Mr.
Wiggins had returned and was amazed to hear
what had happened. And the next day the
younger twins were also intrigued by the story
Bert and Nan told them.

"How exciting to find a thief!" Flossie exclaimed.

This gave Freddie an idea. Running to his room, he rummaged through a bureau drawer until he found a toy sheriff's badge. Pinning it on his chest, he came downstairs and announced proudly that he would be Bert Bobbsey's assistant.

"We'll find the thieves!" he said importantly. "I'll practice right now."

Freddie looked under various pieces of furniture, in the cellar, the attic, behind the garage, and among the bushes. He declared there were no thieves in sight.

"If you want to look for something," Nan told him, when he tired of the game, "how about searching for furniture to put in our ferryboat? We'll need chairs and benches and a table."

"How about the old wicker set up in the attic?" Freddie suggested. "I saw it there a few minutes ago."

"Fine, detective Freddie," Nan told him, and passed the word to their brother and sister.

Together the four children climbed the attic steps. Opening the door, they found an old wicker settee, two chairs, and a footstool. They carried these to the back yard, then scattered to locate anything else which might be used.

Nan saw an old rug in the cellar, and Flossie

located some kitchen chairs which her father had stored over the garage the year before.

"Say, this is great," Freddie said when all the furniture was gathered. "But we don't have a table."

"Let's ask our friends for old furniture," Bert suggested.

So once more the twins went in various directions, this time to the homes of their playmates. It was not long before they were back with a small table, more chairs, and a sofa which Bert had located in Charlie Mason's attic.

"Hurray! Now we're all set!" Freddie cried out.

"But one thing's missing," Nan said, resting her chin in the palm of her hand.

"What's that?" Bert asked.

"A name for our ferryboat. What shall it be?"

Just then Freddie spied their cat Snoop walking over the ridge of the garage roof, and suggested they call the ferryboat the *Snoop*.

"That sounds too much like Danny Rugg," Bert remarked with a chuckle.

A few other names like the *Rover,* the *Sea Lion,* and the *Dolphin* were suggested. But none of them pleased all four twins.

"This must be a unanimous vote," said Bert, and when Freddie and Flossie looked puzzled, he added, "we must all agree on a name."

"When the right name comes along, we'll all know it," said Nan.

Excitement in the Bobbsey home turned from the search for furniture to the prospect of supper at Tara O'Toole's home that evening. Shortly before five o'clock Mrs. Bobbsey called the twins in from the garden for baths and a change of clothes. By six they were ready to leave.

Nan had picked a beautiful bouquet for Mrs. O'Toole. Carrying it, she set off with her brother and sisters for Tara's house. When the Bobbseys arrived Tara presented them to her mother, who came to the door with her. Nan handed the flowers to Mrs. O'Toole and said how happy they were to be supper guests.

"And we are certainly glad you could come," Mrs. O'Toole said with a warm smile. "Now you must meet my mother, and my brother too."

She led the twins into the living room where a beautiful dark-haired woman sat.

"My mother, Madame Lene," Mrs. O'Toole said, then introduced the twins.

Madame Lene looked very charming in her Spanish gypsy costume. She greeted the Bobbseys cordially.

"How happy I am for Tara," said Madame Lene, "that she has such nice friends as you."

"It's lucky for us to have a wonderful friend like Tara," Nan spoke up.

"And this is my uncle Romaine," Tara said, turning to where a tall, very handsome man in a business suit stood smiling.

"It is a great pleasure," Romaine said, "to meet all of you."

He bowed low and shook hands with the Bobbseys. Romaine had jet black hair which was curly at his temples, and flashing eyes equally as black. Nan was especially taken by his friendly smile and gracious manner.

When the introductions were over Freddie could refrain no longer from asking Tara an important question—one which was uppermost in his mind.

"What is your special secret?" he said. "Can we hear about it now?"

"Yes," Flossie piped up, "you have a big surprise for us."

Tara smiled and her dark eyes glowed. Looking at Madame Lene, she asked, "Is it all right to tell them now, Grandmother?"

The gypsy woman nodded. "Yes, my dear," she replied, "you may tell your friends the secret."

CHAPTER XV

AS the twins listened eagerly, Tara said, "My grandmother, Madame Lene, will tell fortunes on the island for one whole day!"

"Oh, how marvelous!" Nan exclaimed, and the other Bobbseys were thrilled too.

"And she'll wear her wonderful headdress," Tara went on. "I'll show it to you!"

She hurried up to her grandmother's bedroom to get the mantilla. When she returned, proudly holding the precious heirloom in her hands, the twins gazed at it in wonder.

The headdress was even more beautiful than they had imagined. Set in the delicate, century-old white lace were glittering gems and shiny gold pieces like the one Tara had worn in her own headdress.

"Oh's" and "Ah's" came from Nan and Flossie as they examined the mantilla more closely. Madame Lene beamed as Flossie cried, "It's bee-yoo-ti-ful!" and Nan gave another sigh of admiration.

"Golly, I've never seen so many tons of money!" was Freddie's breathless comment as he touched a gold piece gingerly.

"And these rubies and sapphires," Bert added. "Madame Lene, your headdress must be worth a great deal of money."

Tara's grandmother smiled and said it was. "But I do not treasure the mantilla only because it is valuable," she added. Her eyes grew dreamy as she continued, "In our gypsy tribe we treasure stories of the past. And my mantilla has a wonderful one, for it belonged originally to my great-great-great grandmother!"

"Please tell us the story," begged Nan, and Madame Lene said she would do this after dinner.

"But first," she said, smiling at Nan and Flossie, "would you both like to try the mantilla on?"

"Oh, yes!" cried Nan.

Madame Lene led both girls toward a low-hanging mirror on the living-room wall. She adjusted the mantilla on Nan, who gazed at herself, speechless.

"You would make a nice little gypsy girl," teased Madame Lene, "with your dark hair and eyes. Maybe I should take you back to Spain!"

Nan laughed and said she would enjoy visiting the country. Impatiently, Flossie said, "Please, may I try the mantilla on now—would I make a good gypsy, too?"

Madame Lene helped Nan take the mantilla off and put it across Flossie's head. "I'm afraid you would never seem gypsyish with your blond curls and big blue eyes," said Madame Lene. "But you look just like a little angel."

"She's a Fat Fairy," Freddie spoke up, and the fortuneteller and her son laughed.

Just then Tara's mother announced that dinner was ready. Freddie was a little nervous about the food, but he soon lost his fears. The onion soup was mild, and the main course of barbecue lamb with tomato and celery sauce was delicious.

During the conversation, Bert and Freddie told about the school project and their ferryboat. Madame Lene and Uncle Romaine were worried to learn about the mysterious person Nan and Bert had chased on Mr. Wiggins' island.

After Uncle Romaine heard about the thieves who had been operating in Lakeport, he frowned. "We must guard the mantilla carefully," he told Madame Lene. "You know how many attempts have already been made to steal it."

"Do not be alarmed," she said. "No one in

Lakeport knows about the mantilla except the Bobbsey family. It will be safe. And now," she continued, when the group had finished a dessert of vanilla walnut pudding, "I'll tell the Bobbseys' fortunes, *si?*"

The twins followed her into the living room where she put on the exquisite mantilla. How radiant she looked in it, Nan thought, as Madame Lene took the girl's hand in hers!

"You are a great comfort to your family," Madame Lene said. "And I see much happiness for you, Nan. Someday you will marry a handsome man and have four lovely children."

Nan smiled. "Will they be two sets of twins?" she asked. Madame Lene said she doubted this, for twins usually skip a generation.

Then the fortuneteller frowned. "Nan, a newcomer in your life will bring someone you know a little bad luck for a while."

Nan gasped and asked, "Who is it, and what can I do to prevent the bad luck, Madame Lene?"

The gypsy took another look at Nan's palm. "I cannot see the mischief-maker's face. But I can see that you will help the person in trouble," she said. "You will do a great service."

The other Bobbseys wondered if the mischief-maker were Danny Rugg or Jack. Bert thought it might be the man they had chased from the island. He vowed to keep on the lookout and try to prevent any trouble.

After Madame Lene had finished telling the fortunes of the other children as well, all of them good, Nan urged her to reveal the story of the headdress.

"It begins with the history of my people in Spain," said the fortuneteller. "By the way, we are called *Gitanos*. It is believed we came originally from Egypt. The *Gitanos* kept to themselves in Spain, wanting to preserve their customs and laws. This aroused the suspicion of the Spaniards and they persecuted our people for many centuries."

"How dreadful!" Nan said. "Did they hurt the poor gypsies very much?"

"Very often," Madame Lene replied, "the *Gitanos* were driven from one part of the country to another. My people were frantic with fear, and some of them, I am afraid, did bad things in return. This did not make them popular.

"During this period my ancestor was born. Her name was also Tara," the gypsy woman said, smiling at her granddaughter. "She became the queen."

"And are you a queen?" Flossie asked her.

"In a way," Madame Lene answered. "I'm called Gypsy Queen of Fortunetellers. Well, Tara grew to be a very beautiful young woman

"I'm called Gypsy Queen of Fortunetellers"

and a talented and graceful dancer as well. By chance she met a handsome Spanish nobleman named Ferdinand, who was from a wealthy and proud family. They fell in love and wished to marry."

Nan spoke up. "And did they?" she asked.

"Yes," said the fortuneteller, "although it was against the law at that time for a gypsy and a pure Spaniard to marry. The couple disobeyed the law and fled to Egypt.

"It was in Egypt," she said, "that the young bridegroom bought this beautiful mantilla for his bride. It was copied from an ancient head-dress of an Egyptian princess. The rubies, the bridegroom said, were like his wife's red lips, and the gold coins represented the sun shining on her pretty face."

"How romantic!" sighed Nan and Tara together.

"Please go on, Madame Lene," Flossie urged.

"Eventually Ferdinand and Tara returned to Spain," Madame Lene continued, "hoping that the King would bestow his good blessings on their marriage. But the King would not forgive them for disobeying his law—he was angry and unrelenting."

"What happened then?" asked Freddie with a worried expression.

Madame Lene said that the nobleman's title

was taken from him and the couple were banished to Egypt.

"Didn't the gypsy tribe try to help them?" asked Bert.

"Yes," said Madame Lene. "Tara sent word to her mother to come, and they would go back with her and live with the gypsies. But when Tara's mother arrived in Egypt she learned it was too late. Tara and her husband had been killed in an accident."

Tears were streaming down Flossie's face as she said, "Oh, how sad!"

"Do not cry, little one," said Madame Lene. "Tara and Ferdinand had left a darling baby girl. The gypsy grandmother brought her and the precious mantilla back to Spain with her. The child grew up and married, and the headdress has been passed on from generation to generation.

"Someday it will go to my daughter Magda," she finished, looking at Mrs. O'Toole. "And then to Tara here."

"That was a wonderful story," said Nan, and the other twins agreed. They thanked Madame Lene for telling it, then asked to hear some more about the gypsies.

"People aren't mean to you any more, are they?" asked Bert.

"Oh, no," Romaine assured him. "One day a

wise king, Charles III, became ruler in Spain. Understanding the problems the gypsies faced, he established new laws and tried to treat our people fairly."

Mrs. O'Toole explained that in modern Spain everyone loves the *Gitanos* because of their colorful songs, dances, and costumes.

"Many Spanish national songs are of gypsy origin," said Mrs. O'Toole, "and so is the music. All the Spaniards consider they are fortunate if they can speak *Calo,* the language of the gypsies. And there are many gypsy words in the Spanish language."

Freddie now looked at Tara's uncle. "Will you show us how you fight bulls?" he asked.

Uncle Romaine laughed. Then he got up, bowed low, and said, "Certainly. I will be honored to tell you anything about the sport you would like to know."

"And would you play bullfighter with me?" Freddie asked, his eyes shining happily.

An amused look came over Uncle Romaine's face. "You mean, you would like to make believe that you are a bull?"

"Yes," said Freddie, "and you'll be the matador. Look, I'm the bull!" Saying this, the small boy held his hands to the sides of his head with a finger on each pointing up like horns.

Flossie giggled. "You look more like a goat!"

Freddie ignored this and said to Uncle Romaine, "I'll try to buck you!"

As the others looked on smiling, Uncle Romaine asked to be excused for a few minutes. When he returned, the Bobbseys gasped, for the fine-looking man was dressed in his bullfighting matador costume. He wore tight black leggings, a beautiful red vest and sash, fancy, ruffled white shirt, and a tricorn hat. The yellow cape he carried over his arm was covered with embroidery.

"And now, my young bull friend," he said, "do your best to catch me. Or else I'll catch you."

Everybody stood back while Freddie Bobbsey, still holding his "horns" erect, hunched his shoulders and dashed at the matador. Uncle Romaine twirled his cape and stepped aside. Freddie merely butted the air. Again and again the boy tried different maneuvers, but each time the graceful matador sidestepped him.

"Now you know how the bull feels," Romaine said, smiling.

Freddie puffed and looked sheepish at not having been able to run into the matador. He would give one final lunge, he decided.

Putting his head down, Freddie dashed toward Uncle Romaine once more. The matador leaped to one side, flicking his cape before Freddie's eyes. The boy could not see where he was going.

Across the room he plunged, straight toward a table on which stood a beautiful vase. *Crash*— he ran right into it! The table teetered, and the tall vase flew through the air! But with a graceful leap the matador caught the vase in his arms just in the nick of time.

"Oh!" cried Freddie.

"No harm done, young man," Romaine told him as everyone cheered.

"I guess I'm not a good bull after all," Freddie said as he sat down again. The matador assured him he had done very well. "There is an art to bullfighting," he said. "One must tease the animal in such a way that he becomes playful."

"But doesn't break vases," Bert grinned.

Nan, who had been admiring Romaine's outfit, asked him to show them some of the prescribed movements of a matador. Romaine obligingly went through a few, stepping forward, backward, and to the side with the grace of a dancer.

"Oh, how lovely!" Nan sighed. Then she stood up, saying the Bobbseys had had a wonderful evening and must go home now. "It has been such fun hearing the stories about gypsies," she said. "Even the one about the cruel kings. And

Madame Lene, it's so kind of you to offer to tell fortunes for a day on the island, and wear the headdress."

Flossie, who had been very quiet, said, "She'll be our Gypsy Queen of Fortunetellers." Then suddenly the little girl's eyes opened very wide and she cried out:

"I know the best name in all the world for our ferryboat. The *Gypsy Queen!*"

CHAPTER XVI

"HELP!"

FLOSSIE'S sudden announcement startled everyone for a moment. Then they laughed and agreed one by one that *Gypsy Queen* would be an excellent name for the little ferryboat.

"She'll be the Queen of Lake Metoka," said Nan.

"In a red dress," Freddie spoke up. "But she ought to have a crown. I'll make one out of flowers and put it on the pilot house."

"And I'll be the king and hold her wheel-arm," said Bert.

The gaiety continued for several moments, then the twins sobered. Madame Lene thanked the Bobbseys for the honor of having the boat named after her.

Romaine added, "Just for that, I shall play some gypsy tunes on my violin before you leave."

There was so much rhythm in the gypsy melodies that all the children danced and sang songs for another half hour. Finally they said good night.

As the twins were being driven home by Tara's mother, Nan said, "Let's paint the name on the ferryboat tomorrow morning."

"Oh, yes!" the others chorused.

"And maybe we can take our first passengers to the island," Bert remarked eagerly.

"Good luck," said Mrs. O'Toole as she pulled up in front of the Bobbsey house.

"I'll come down and help you," Tara offered.

Right after breakfast next morning, Bert went to buy a can of gold paint. The other children packed various articles in the station wagon, including the wicker furniture and rug from the attic. Freddie also insisted upon taking his toy fire engine which squirted water.

"That's quite an affair," remarked Mr. Wiggins, who was helping the children load the car. "So you're a little fireman."

"Yes, I am. But my engine pumps a big stream," Freddie said proudly.

Soon everything was ready. Mr. Wiggins and the children climbed aboard. Mrs. Bobbsey, who was already at the wheel, drove directly to the little ferryboat.

"Nan, you sketch the name on the pilot

house," Bert suggested as they stepped out on the dock. "Then I'll help you paint it."

His twin smiled and nodded as Bert picked up the can of paint and two brushes he had brought. Nan carefully outlined the words, *Gypsy Queen.* Then the two children painted them in gold letters. Nan took the front and Bert the rear of the pilot house.

Later, as the Bobbseys stood back to admire the work, Mrs. Bobbsey said, "We really should christen the *Gypsy Queen.*"

"You mean break a bottle over the front of the boat?" Nan asked.

Mrs. Bobbsey said they did not have a bottle. Before anyone could offer to go for one, Freddie said, "I have an idea!" He ran into the cabin where he had put his red fire engine. When he brought it out, Flossie said, "How can a fire engine christen a boat?"

"I'll show you." Her twin ran down to the water's edge and filled the fire engine's tank with water. Hurrying back, he said, "We'll squirt the water of Lake Metoka on the bow of the boat to christen her."

Mrs. Bobbsey laughed but said this would do nicely. "We're all set," she called, and everyone gathered on the deck at the front of the boat.

Squirt, squirt, squirt!

Freddie's fire engine threw a small stream of

water down on the bow as Nan announced, "We christen thee *Gypsy Queen.*"

By this time several curious onlookers, both children and adults, had gathered on the dock and they clapped when the little ferryboat received its name.

Mr. Wiggins' face wore a wide grin. "I hardly recognize my old cattleboat," he said. "The *Gypsy Queen* sure is pretty."

Suddenly the honking of a horn caused everyone to turn around. Driving up to the dock was a truck from Mr. Bobbsey's lumberyard, with Sam at the wheel. The truck was loaded with the furniture the twins had collected from their friends for the cabin of the ferryboat. The children carried the pieces onto the boat, and when the chairs and settees were in place, the *Gypsy Queen* resembled a comfortable yacht.

"It's right nice," said Sam. "And I have something your dad sent for the ferryboat rides. How do you like these?" From the front of the truck, he pulled out several rolls of colored tickets and metal boxes for money.

"Why, this is just what we'll need on the boat and at the island," Nan exclaimed.

"And here's another surprise," came a girl's voice. Everyone turned around.

"Nellie Parks! What are those?" Nan called, seeing her friend walking toward the dock with an armful of large pieces of cardboard.

"They're posters," Nellie replied. "I made them to advertise what we're doing."

"They're bee-yoo-ti-ful," Flossie burst out, as Nellie displayed the lovely drawings and lettering in red, green, white, and blue paint. The pictures showed the merry-go-round, slides, swings, and fortunetelling tent as well as the ferryboat.

Suddenly Nellie spied the newly painted name. "Say, that's great," she said. "I'll add that to the posters."

"We'll put them in store windows today," Bert said, "and start our ferryboat passenger service tomorrow."

That afternoon he and Nan, along with Charlie Mason and Nellie Parks, rode their bicycles around town, placing the posters in various shops. At each place boys and girls who saw the ads wanted to buy tickets for the outing immediately.

"They'll be on sale at the dock," Nan told them. "First come, first served."

Everyone seemed delighted with the project except Danny Rugg and Jack Westley, whom the twins met as they were placing one sign in a supermarket.

"Who cares about your old boat?" Jack said, sneering.

"That island playground is just for sissy kids," Danny added.

The Bobbseys and their friends paid no attention to the rude boys.

"It's for babies!" Danny hooted as they went on their way to place a poster in the corner drugstore.

But by nine the next morning Aunt Sue Smith's dock was crowded with youngsters. Nan and Flossie were busy selling tickets, while Bert and Freddie, assisted by Charlie, stood by to show the young passengers and the parents of small children where to sit or stand on the ferryboat.

Grace Levine was the first person to buy a ticket from Flossie. She was followed by Tara, who wore her gypsy costume and was ready for her palm reading on the island. Others came aboard quickly.

Presently a boy on shore called, "How many people will your ferryboat carry?"

Flossie answered quickly, "As many people as twelve cows and six goats!"

Everyone howled with laughter and Nan said, "I think a cow is equal to six children."

When the ferryboat was nearly full, Mr. Wiggins called down from the pilot house, "No more passengers, please. We have enough for the first trip."

Suddenly a boy's voice called out, "Hey, I want a ride, too!"

"Same here," called another lad, and Danny and Jack raced up to the ticket table. They were followed by four other friends of theirs.

"I'm afraid we can't take any more," Nan said.

"Oh, trying to keep us out, eh?" Danny snapped.

Flossie looked up to the pilot house, "Mr. Wiggins, can we take another cow?" she asked.

"What does Flossie mean by that?" Jack scowled as Nellie giggled.

Nan explained as Mr. Wiggins replied that he was afraid of overloading the boat. But he said, if the newcomers would divide their number equally on either side of the *Gypsy Queen,* it would be all right.

"See, you couldn't keep us out," Danny said with a triumphant grin as he bought the tickets.

When Danny and his five friends boarded the boat, Bert said, "Three of you go on one side and three on the other."

"Says who! My friends and I will go where we want to!"

The six boys ran to the far side of the boat and as they did the ferryboat began to list.

"Divide!" Mr. Wiggins called sternly.

Not understanding, several of the children on the other side ran to where Danny and his friends were standing.

"We have too many on board. Get off, Danny!"

"Get back!" Mr. Wiggins cried. The boys and girls obeyed but the pilot called down, "We have too many on board. The last six must get off!"

This made Danny and his friends furious. They stomped off the boat as Flossie refunded their money.

Now the boat was balanced perfectly and Mr. Wiggins started the engine. As the *Gypsy Queen* pulled away from the dock Danny shouted, "You kids are stupid. The Bobbseys are making this money to keep for themselves!"

"That's not so!" Nan called back.

Nellie Parks put an arm around her friend and told her not to worry about what Danny said. "Nobody believes him anyway," she said kindly.

Danny's rudeness was soon forgotten as the *Gypsy Queen* carried the happy children toward the island. When they arrived, the two policemen on guard met the boat. As the passengers went ashore, Bert spoke to the officers.

"Any sign of that prowler?" he asked.

"There's been nothing suspicious here," one of the men reported. Then he smiled. "From the looks of this happy crowd, I'd say your project is going to be a great success today."

The policeman's prediction proved to be true. Everyone had a jolly time on the merry-go-round, swings, slides, in Tara's tent, and eating the lunches they had brought. Nan and Nellie sold cookies and soft drinks. Mr. Bobbsey came over in a motorboat to see how everything was working out. He brought Waggo, and immediately Freddie had the dog perform his tricks, charging a penny for people to see them.

By the time the ferryboat had to depart, the Bobbseys had collected a good bit of money for their school project. Nan counted it on the way back to Lakeport.

"Oh, Bert, this is wonderful," she said. "And I know we'll make even more on the day when Madame Lene tells fortunes."

News of the project's success spread rapidly through Lakeport. As a result, twice as many children and many adults crowded around the dock Monday morning. Bert announced that they would make two trips that day. Finally, the day arrived when Madame Lene was to tell fortunes. A great crowd was waiting as Tara and her family boarded the ferry. In addition, people in motorboats and a few in canoes already were heading toward the island.

Soon the *Gypsy Queen* was filled to capacity for the first trip. *Toot, toot!* went the ferry's horn and the boat started across the lake.

After it had docked, Bert, Freddie, and Charlie Mason set up a special tent for Madame Lene's fortunetelling. It was large, and inside were flowers and pictures. It was not long before a long line of boys, girls, and grownups had formed in front of it.

Tara sat outside the tent, selling tickets. When she had kept at her task for an hour, Nan Bobbsey ran up to the girl.

"Tara, why don't you have some fun on the swings," she suggested, "while I get another girl to sell tickets?"

"I would love to," Tara admitted.

Nan hurried away but returned soon with Susie Larker, who had agreed to take over the ticket selling. Nan said that Nellie Parks was taking charge of the cooky table, so Nan would go with Tara. The two chums ran off to enjoy the rides together.

"How wonderful this is!" Tara exclaimed some time later. "But I guess I'd better go back to Grandmother's tent now."

"All right, I'll go with you," Nan offered.

The friends took one more ride on the swings, then hurried back to relieve Susie Larker. As they drew near the tent, the girls noticed that no one was there now except Susie. But they could hear angry words coming from inside the fortuneteller's booth.

A man's voice was saying, "This is all tommyrot! You have no right to put such ideas into my wife's head!"

As the two girls stared at each other dumfounded, there came the sound of a tussle from inside. Before Nan and Tara could look into the tent, a woman rushed out, followed by a man. Tara recognized them immediately.

"They're the ones who wanted to buy my head-dress at the school fair!" she whispered to Nan.

The two girls, fearful, dashed inside the tent. A moment later Tara screamed:

"Help! Help!"

Madame Lene lay on the floor, moaning.

CHAPTER XVII

SPEEDY ESCAPE

"GRANDMOTHER! Grandmother!" Tara said, bending over Madame Lene.

"Let's help her into this chair," Nan said. "Then we must get a doctor!"

The fortuneteller was moaning and muttering in Spanish-gypsy language. Tara said she was saying something about "suspicious hands."

At this moment Bert, Freddie, and Flossie, attracted by the commotion, hurried in. Flossie cried out that she had seen the bad man and woman running away.

"Get a doctor, Bert, quick!" Nan ordered.

Bert replied that he had just seen Dr. Lawrence in the crowd. He would go for him immediately.

"And you, Freddie," Nan continued, "get the policeman!"

A moment after the two boys had left, Flossie said, "Where's Madame Lene's headdress?"

For the first time the others realized it was not on the fortuneteller's head. And it was not in sight.

Nan uttered a stifled cry. "The mantilla! It's gone!"

This was too much for Tara. With her grandmother injured and the heirloom stolen, the little girl burst into tears and sobbed as if her heart would break.

Nan tried to comfort her friend, but she kept wondering what Madame Lene had meant by "suspicious hands." Were they the hands of the couple who had just fled? Was this the bad luck that had been predicted by the fortuneteller herself?

As the girl rubbed the gypsy's wrists and gently stroked her forehead, Dr. Lawrence arrived.

"Oh, my grandmother seems terribly ill," Tara told him. "Please do something for her right away!"

The doctor patted her shoulder reassuringly and asked the girls to wait outside while he examined Madame Lene.

In a few moments Freddie came with the policeman. Romaine was with them. Nan quickly told the officer about the couple in the tent and the missing heirloom.

"We may be able to catch the thieves before they leave the island," the policeman said. "Come on! We'll make a search!"

The officer, Bert, Nan, and Romaine dashed away from the fortuneteller's tent. The small twins and Tara remained in case they should be needed. Not knowing where to look first, the men and boys asked several bystanders if they had seen the fleeing couple.

"I saw them run over that way," a boy said, pointing toward the opposite side of the island.

"I did too," called a woman.

Hurrying as fast as they could through the bushes and over the stones in the woods, the searching party reached the beach on the far side of the island. They were just in time to see a speedboat turning out of a cove.

"We're too late!" Nan exclaimed, her heart sinking.

In the boat sat a pilot and a blond man and woman.

"Are they the ones?" the policeman asked. "They must have waded out."

"Yes," Nan replied.

The couple crouched low on the seat in order to hide their faces, but Nan had recognized them.

"We must stop them!" Bert cried as the speedboat circled around the end of the island and headed toward Lakeport.

"We'll do it!" said the policeman. "But we'll have to go back to the dock. And I'll radio headquarters too."

When they reached the playground area, the policeman got out his short-wave set from a tent and contacted headquarters. With Nan's help he gave a description of the couple and asked that they be caught and questioned.

While the officer was busy, Nan and Romaine ran back to the tent to find out about Madame Lene. Tara said the doctor was still with her. But he had told Tara that her grandmother was not severely injured. She was suffering mainly from shock, due to the theft of the valuable mantilla.

Nan and Romaine dashed to the dock where Bert was waiting. He had asked a man with a speedy motorboat if he would help them, should the policeman need him.

"Glad to," the man replied and started the motor.

Presently the officer came rushing to the shore and said he would be glad to borrow the boat. "My name's Hancock," he said.

"And mine's Wallace," the pilot told them. "Jump in."

The twins, Romaine, and the officer climbed into the motorboat, which started off with a zip as a crowd of onlookers gaped in astonishment.

"Where to?" Mr. Wallace asked.

"Toward Lakeport," Officer Hancock answered. "But I don't know which dock. Children, keep your eyes open for that couple."

The motor hummed. The race was on. But the suspects' getaway speedboat had a long head-start, and the pursuers did not see it. Presently they came upon the police launch making a search.

"Haven't spotted that couple yet," an officer called to Hancock.

"We haven't either. They've probably gone ashore already."

Taking opposite sides of the lake, the two boats went on. Finally Bert saw a speedboat just coming from a dock. Only a pilot was in it, but the boy yelled excitedly:

"It looks like the one that couple was in!"

Their own pilot raced after the speedboat toward Lakeport. Just as it docked once more at the northern end of Lakeport, the pursuers caught up to it. The man at the wheel was undoubtedly the one who had taken the blond couple from the island. Officer Hancock started to question him at once.

"Where did your passengers go?" the policeman demanded, as his pilot pulled alongside the speedboat.

"My passengers? Why, I don't know."

"We think they're thieves!" the policeman told him. "Who are they?"

"Never saw 'em before today. They didn't give their names."

The speedboat owner said that he had been engaged by the couple to take them over to the island, wait, and bring them back again. "I think they're strangers in town," he said.

"They stole a very valuable mantilla from Madame Lene!" Nan burst out.

"What!" the man exclaimed.

"You didn't see it?" Bert asked.

"No."

Officer Hancock thought that perhaps one of the couple had hidden the headdress under a coat. He checked the speedboat owner's identity to satisfy himself that he was not in league with the thieves. Seeing his license, he recognized him as a retired Lakeport merchant.

The policeman now hopped ashore, asking the others to wait for him. He said he wanted to phone headquarters and make a report.

"The launch may as well return," he added.

Nan spoke up. "Couldn't it go to the island and bring Madame Lene back? I'm sure she'll want to return home."

"I'll suggest it," Hancock offered.

When he came back, he said the launch would head directly for the island. Then the twins and the others in the motorboat started for the play-ground too.

As they skimmed across the water, Bert asked the officer what the chances were for locating the valuable, jeweled headdress that had been stolen. Hancock shrugged, but said the police would certainly try hard to locate it.

"What I'm afraid of," he added, "is that the thieves may remove the stones and coins and sell them."

"Madame Lene will be heartbroken," Nan murmured.

As soon as they reached the island, all of them hurried to the fortuneteller's tent. To their delight, they found that Tara's grandmother was much better although she was still overcome with shock at the loss of the priceless heirloom. All expressed their sympathy, saying they hoped it would soon be recovered.

"Would you like to go home now?" Nan asked her. "The police will take you in their launch."

"Oh, thank you," she said. Dr. Lawrence thought this was a good idea and said he would go along.

Romaine and Tara helped Madame Lene to the boat and said they would accompany her back to Lakeport.

"May I go with them, please, Nan?" asked Freddie.

She was about to say no when Romaine spoke up and said, "Come along, boy. I will take you to your house."

Freddie hopped into the launch and it pulled away from the dock. After that the fun on the island seemed to slow down. Madame Lene's bad luck had cast a gloom over the gathering, so Bert and Nan decided to close their project earlier than they had the day before.

When the playground apparatus had been put in order, and all papers and trash cleaned up, the visitors filed back onto the *Gypsy Queen,* and set off across the lake. On the way they met the police launch coming back to the island with half a dozen officers aboard.

"Ahoy there!" Flossie called, trying to act like a lady sea captain.

"Ahoy yourself!" Lieutenant Pyle shouted back, as he shut off the motor and let the launch drift alongside the ferryboat. "Any sign of the missing mantilla?"

"Not on the island," Bert called. "Have you had any luck tracing the thieves?"

"No," the officer replied. "They seem to have vanished. But our detectives are working hard on the case," he assured them, adding that he was taking extra police to the island, not only as guards but to be there in case the blond couple should show up.

"If they return we'll be ready for them," Lieutenant Pyle said. He started the motor, and the launch continued across the lake.

Shortly afterward the *Gypsy Queen* landed at the Smiths' dock and the passengers started off.

"I'll see you tomorrow," Flossie said, waving good-by to the Bobbseys' friends who were helping with the project.

"We guarantee there'll be no more thieves to bother us," Bert declared, smiling.

Charlie Mason's father was waiting for him at the dock and offered to take the Bobbseys and Mr. Wiggins home.

"Thank you, Mr. Mason," Nan said, and helped Flossie into the car. Then she stepped in herself, carrying the money boxes and a roll of tickets.

"Don't mention it," Charlie's father replied, whereupon Bert introduced the two men, and they started off.

"You and the Bobbseys certainly are doing a grand job," Mr. Mason said to Mr. Wiggins as they drove along.

Soon they were in front of the Bobbsey home. The twins found Dinah and Sam in the kitchen, dancing around the room joyfully.

"Dinah won the contest!" Sam exclaimed gleefully. "The *Times* newspaper picture contest!"

" 'Deed I did," said Dinah proudly.

"Oh, that's wonderful!" cried the children.

"We're both goin' to Washington," Dinah said, grinning and rolling her eyes toward Sam. "And now, I'd better stop this celebratin' and put the soup on the table."

At supper the family discussed the exciting events of the day. While they were eating dessert, Freddie suddenly spoke up, saying he had something to tell. "I have the biggest secret in the world!"

"What is it, little Fat Fireman?" Mr. Bobbsey asked.

Freddie shook his head. "I'm not telling anybody 'cept Flossie." The two younger twins put their heads together for a moment and both began to giggle.

Before going to bed that evening, Nan telephoned to Tara and asked how Madame Lene was feeling.

"Grandmother is much better," Tara told Nan. "But she won't really be happy again until she finds the precious mantilla." Then Tara added, "Did Freddie tell you his secret?"

"No," said Nan, "he only told Flossie."

"I don't know it, either," Tara confessed. "It's between Freddie and Uncle Romaine."

The following morning Bert called police headquarters as soon as he had dressed. He was disappointed to learn that not a trace of the thieves had been found either in Lakeport or on the island.

Flossie and Freddie had the giggles all morning. Even on their way to the island, the younger twins exchanged sideways glances in anticipation of the secret. But they would tell no one what it was.

Then, at two o'clock in the afternoon, Flossie and Freddie went to the pilot house of the *Gypsy Queen* and tooted the whistle. As a crowd gathered to learn what the excitement was about, the little boy announced in as deep a voice as he could manage:

"Ladee-es and gentlemen! The bullfighting-est fighter you ever saw will now show us how he handles a bull."

Freddie tooted the ship's horn again and added, "Look over there, ladies and gentlemen!"

He pointed to Madame Lene's fortunetelling tent on the island. Out of it stepped Romaine, wearing his tight-fitting velvet suit, tricorn hat, and red silk scarf.

"A real bullfighter!" several onlookers said in astonishment.

A moment later Romaine reached into the tent and led out a small bull calf. This time the crowd set up a howl of delight.

Bert and Nan were astounded. As Flossie and Freddie joined the older twins, Bert asked,

"How did you ever get the calf over here?"

"We snuggled him," Flossie said.

"She means smuggled," Freddie said importantly. Then he explained that Romaine had brought the calf over during the night, with the assistance of the policemen who were guarding the island.

"And now, for the greatest show of all," Freddie announced. "My sister Flossie has the tickets."

After everybody had paid ten cents apiece, Romaine took his voluminous cape and waved it in front of the calf. The baby bull dodged this way and that, becoming very much annoyed that it could not hit the flying cape.

"Oh, this is wonderful!" cried Charlie Mason.

The calf tried to gallop off, but Freddie and Mr. Wiggins shooed it back. The audience howled with laughter when they saw this. Once more the little bull tried to get away. For the second time Freddie chased it back toward Romaine.

By now the calf had had enough of such nonsense. Turning and lowering his head, he made a beeline for Freddie!

CHAPTER XVIII

A JOYFUL DAY

FLOSSIE screamed as the bull calf charged toward her twin brother.

"Stop him!" she shouted, and the other children screamed in fright.

At first little Freddie was so scared that he could not move. But he recovered quickly and began to dodge. First he dashed to the left. When the bull veered to that side, Freddie dodged to the right. But the calf would not be fooled. Lowering his head, he aimed directly for the helpless boy.

All this time Romaine had been watching intently. Nan noticed this and was sure he would not let the bull calf hurt Freddie.

Now Romaine dashed forward and swung his cape. The calf turned his head to one side, taking his eye off Freddie for an instant. With lightning speed Romaine threw his cape to the ground and leaped through the air toward the animal.

As the crowd gasped in awe, the matador threw his arms about the bull's neck and gave him a quick flip. The bull fell to the ground, just a foot from Freddie.

Everybody cheered the matador, who now lay atop the panting calf. Romaine leaped gracefully to his feet and helped the animal get up.

"You shouldn't play so rough," he scolded, and gave the calf a spanking, which made everybody laugh.

"Thank you, Uncle Romaine," Freddie said, walking up and shaking the man's hand. "I hope you didn't hurt him."

But the young bull was none the worse for his spill. In fact, he seemed rather contrite, his big brown eyes looking sadly into Freddie's. Then, without warning, he flicked out his tongue and licked the little boy's arm in a gesture of friendship.

"He didn't mean to frighten you," Romaine said as he patted the calf.

"Can we go on with the show?" Freddie asked.

"Of course."

Now Romaine put on a very graceful act with the young bull, which charged into the swirling cape until his spindly legs grew tired. After the make-believe bullfight was over, Romaine tethered the animal to a near-by tree, and Bert brought him a bucket of water from the lake.

The excitement had hardly died down, when one of the police guards, named Wooley, hurried over, carrying a two-way pocket radio in his hands. "I have a message for the Bobbsey twins and Tara O'Toole," he announced.

"Oh, is it about Grandmother?" Tara asked fearfully. "Is she worse?"

"No. It's news about those thieves," the officer said, smiling.

"Tell us, please," Nan begged, as the children gathered around.

"I just received a radio message from police headquarters saying that the two suspects have been arrested!"

"Wow!" Bert exclaimed. "Tell us more."

"Who were they?" Nan asked, excited.

"The couple gave their names as Horace and Gertrude Trevor," Wooley said, "and they were caught in a boardinghouse in Lakeport." Then he paused and smiled. "The chief said to thank the Bobbsey twins for giving him the good clue with the number 24 on it."

The officer explained that the couple had been found at 24 York Street. "They checked every house numbered 24 until they found the right one," he said.

"And what about the heel prints?" Bert asked.

"That was the clue which broke the case," Wooley answered. "Horace Trevor wore Lion's Head rubber heels. When the chief showed him the picture of the prints you found in the sand, the man finally confessed."

As the Bobbseys' friends gathered around to hear the details of the arrest, the policeman said that the Trevors had been in the neighborhood about a month. They had robbed several stores and amassed a lot of cash, which they wanted to hide.

"Oh, that's why the bad man had so much money in his wallet!" Flossie blurted, recalling the scene in Tara's tent on the afternoon of the school fair.

"Exactly," the officer agreed. "And that's why they came to this island—to hide the loot."

He added that the two hundred dollars which the Bobbseys had found was part of the stolen money and would be returned to the rightful owners, along with some stolen jewelry.

"Then Grandmother's mantilla was recovered," Tara said, sighing with relief.

Officer Wooley looked at her sadly. "I'm sorry to say it wasn't."

"They didn't have it?" Bert exclaimed, aghast.

"The police searched everywhere," the officer said, "but did not find the mantilla."

"The Trevors took it!" Nan exclaimed. "I'm sure of that."

"That's one thing they deny," Wooley said.

"Then why did they hurt Grandmother?" Tara asked angrily.

The officer said that Horace Trevor claimed Madame Lene frightened his wife by telling her she would get into serious trouble, so he had shoved the gypsy, and she fell down. "But he insists they did not take the mantilla."

"Are you certain the headdress was nowhere in their room?" Nan asked.

"Yes," said the policeman. "Our men looked everywhere, but there was no sign of it."

"Maybe they've sold it," Bert suggested. But Wooley did not think the two had had time to dispose of anything so valuable.

Suddenly Nan said, "Maybe they hid the

mantilla on this island before they escaped!"

Wooley looked at her in amazement. This was one possibility the police had not considered.

Tara became very excited. "You may be right, Nan!" she cried. "Let's take a look."

"Come on!" Bert's voice rang out.

The twins, along with Tara and the policeman, began to scour the small island again. The first place they headed for was the spot where Nan had found the bag of money. But there was nothing to indicate any further digging.

Bert frowned thoughtfully for a few minutes, then he had an idea. In his mind he laid out an imaginary line from Madame Lene's tent to the cove where the Trevors had escaped in the speedboat. Walking carefully along the route, he directed the children to look right and left. But there was still no sign of anything unusual that might point to the mantilla.

"Oh dear," Tara sighed as they neared the sandy beach. "I'm afraid those thieves didn't hide the headdress here on the island, Nan."

"Don't be too sure," Nan replied, as her keen eyes noticed something. "See that strange-looking bush!" she exclaimed.

"What do you mean?" Bert asked.

"The leaves are limp and shriveled," Nan replied, "as if the bush were just stuck into the ground without being rooted."

As the amazed policeman looked on, Bert yanked the bush out of the ground easily.

"It's a fake plant," Freddie cried.

The children could see that the branches apparently had been cut from a larger bush near by, because there were no roots on the stems.

"But why would anybody do that?" Tara wondered.

"Possibly as a marker," Bert surmised, as he and Nan dropped to their knees to examine the ground.

"It's all been dug up here," Nan said, sifting the loose soil between her fingers. "I'll bet something's buried underneath."

With Bert's help, Nan dug a large hole. Suddenly she cried out, "There's a box down here!"

She scraped aside some sand to uncover the top of a cardboard container.

"Oh, I hope—I hope—" Tara whispered as Bert lifted the box to the surface.

Nan quickly removed the top. Inside was the stolen mantilla!

"You don't have to hope any more," Bert said as Tara jubilantly clutched the heirloom, which glistened in the sunlight.

"Now I know Grandmother will get well in a hurry!" Tara exclaimed. "How can I ever thank you Bobbseys?" she asked, giving Nan a hug.

All the twins smiled with pleasure, and Nan

said, "When you read my palm and said there was going to be great excitement in store for me, you didn't know you'd have it also. And Madame Lene didn't realize she would too."

Tara admitted this was true. She had been so busy telling other peoples' fortune that she had completely forgotten to learn what might be in store for herself.

"But if we all really knew what was going to happen to us, it wouldn't be such fun," Nan said, and the others agreed.

Officer Wooley said there was one thing everybody could be sure about—the Bobbseys certainly were good detectives. "And speaking of that," he said, "I'd better radio a report to headquarters."

The children listened happily as he carried on a two-way talk with the chief in Lakeport. When Wooley finished he said the chief wanted to speak to them.

"You children did a grand job," he said.

"Will you tell my grandmother right away that we found her mantilla?" Tara asked him.

"We sure will."

After the chief signed off, the Bobbseys hurried across the island to tell the good news to their playmates. When the crowd heard about their detective work, a great cheer went up. Now everyone was happier than ever.

An hour later they were surprised to see a

police launch arriving. In it were Madame Lene and Tara's mother.

"After the wonderful news, we couldn't stay away," said the fortuneteller. Then, as Nan handed her the mantilla, Madame Lene said, "What can I do to repay you for what you have done? Tell me please. Perhaps there is something in my native Spain you would like—"

Nan, Bert, and the small twins shook their heads at once. "We were glad to do it," said Nan.

"But surely there is some little thing," Romaine insisted.

"I know," Flossie spoke up. "You can play your violin for us some time so Tara and her mother can dance for us."

The gypsy and his sister laughed and said this would indeed give them pleasure. It was arranged that on the last day of the island playground there would be a gala celebration. It would include the dancing.

In just two more days the Bobbseys' project had earned the needed money. For the closing hours the *Gypsy Queen* made several trips and the island was crowded. Romaine brought his violin. Madame Lene wore her mantilla, while Tara and her mother were in Spanish dancing costumes.

Romaine lifted his bow, and soon the air was filled with lively notes, as Tara and her mother did a Spanish flamenco dance. How they tossed their heads and swirled their full skirts as the music grew faster and faster! All the children and adults cheered loudly.

When the dance ended, there was a long blast of the ferryboat's horn. Everyone looked up to see Mr. Wiggins, who was standing in the pilot house.

"Jeepers, do we have to go home already?" Teddy Blake asked, disappointed.

"It's not time yet," Susie replied, glancing at her wrist watch.

"Don't worry, folks," Mr. Wiggins called out. "We're not shoving off. Mr. Tetlow would like to say a few words to you all."

The school principal, smiling, walked to the edge of the ferryboat's deck. All the merry-makers pressed close to hear what he had to say.

"Friends," he began, "the island project has been a tremendous success. There is already more money than we will need for modernizing the school stage. In fact, there will be enough money left for new equipment on the school playground."

Great shouts went up from the boys and girls when they heard this. Then Mr. Tetlow called the Bobbsey twins to the deck beside him, and shook their hands. "We owe this fine idea to you and your playmates who helped. And I personally want to thank Mr. Wiggins, who gave you this wonderful ferryboat."

Following Mr. Tetlow's speech, Police Lieutenant Pyle came aboard. He said that he had come to the island to take his men back to Lakeport.

"We are no longer needed here," he said, "because the Bobbseys have solved the mystery of the stolen mantilla. Yet there are certain things I would like to clear up for you."

The officer explained that the Trevors were experts on the value of old gold coins. "They came to Lakeport to steal," he said, "and happened to spot the gold coin on Tara's headdress at the school fair. Knowing it was of great worth, they tried to buy it but failed.

"Then they spied on Tara to find out where she lived. They even followed her to the Bobbseys' home on the day she taught them fortune-telling.

"And when they finally learned where Tara lived," Pyle continued, "the Trevors became eavesdroppers. They overheard talk about Madame Lene's famous mantilla and decided to steal it."

Then the officer said the Trevors had finally confessed that they had hidden the mantilla on the island, with the hope of coming back to dig it up some day. "Now," Pyle concluded, "I think we should all give the Bobbsey Twins three cheers!"

When the shouting died down, Flossie's small voice was heard to say, "We should thank our lovely *Gypsy Queen,* too. She's the bestest boat in the whole wide world!"

Flossie patted the sides of the cabin as the cheers rose again. And Mr. Wiggins tooted the horn in response.

The children wondered if they ever again would become so excited about any adventure. But the Bobbsey Twins were soon to have a great deal of fun and excitement at Pilgrim Rock.

At this point Charlie Mason ran to the deck and called out, "I've had a swell time here. If the Bobbseys and Mr. Wiggins will do it, how many of you want the island playground to last all summer?"

"We do! We do!" all the boys and girls responded.

The twins smiled and said they would be glad to lend the boat. They looked toward Mr. Wiggins.

He nodded. "I'll run the *Gypsy Queen.*"

"But what'll we do with all the money?" Freddie asked.

Nan had a ready answer. "We can give it to the children's hospital in Lakeport."

"Great! Swell! Keen!" came the happy cries.

Farmer Wiggins beamed at his young friends. "It used to be fun running this boat for my cattle, but it's a lot more fun running it as the *Gypsy Queen*."

"Do you know," said Flossie, looking at the Bobbseys' own little ferryboat, then at Tara, her mother, Romaine, and Madame Lene, "I just love all kinds of gypsies!"

Grinning, her twin gave three tugs on the horn of the little ferryboat.

ORDER FORM

BOBBSEY TWINS ADVENTURE SERIES

Now that you've met the Bobbsey Twins, we're sure you'll want to "accompany" them on other exciting adventures. So for your convenience, we've enclosed this handy order form.

42 TITLES AT YOUR BOOKSELLER OR COMPLETE AND MAIL THIS HANDY COUPON TO:

GROSSET & DUNLAP, INC.
P.O. Box 941, Madison Square Post Office, New York, N.Y. 10010
Please send me the Bobbsey Twins Adventure Book(s) checked below @ $1.95 each, plus 25¢ *per book* postage and handling. My check or money order for $_____ is enclosed.

☐ 1. Of Lakeport	8001-X	
☐ 2. Adventure in the Country	8002-8	
☐ 3. Secret at the Seashore	8003-6	
☐ 4. Mystery at School	8004-4	
☐ 5. At Snow Lodge	8005-2	
☐ 6. On A Houseboat	8006-0	
☐ 7. Mystery at Meadowbrook	8007-9	
☐ 8. Big Adventure at Home	8008-7	
☐ 9. Search in the Great City	8009-5	
☐ 10. On Blueberry Island	8010-9	
☐ 11. Mystery on the Deep Blue Sea	8011-7	
☐ 12. Adventure in Washington	8012-5	
☐ 13. Visit to the Great West	8013-3	
☐ 14. And the Cedar Camp Mystery	8014-1	
☐ 15. And the County Fair Mystery	8015-X	
☐ 16. Camping Out	8016-8	
☐ 17. Adventures With Baby May	8017-6	
☐ 18. And the Play House Secret	8018-4	
☐ 19. And the Four-Leaf Clover Mystery	8019-2	
☐ 20. The Mystery at Cherry Corners	8020-6	
☐ 24. Wonderful Winter Secret	8024-9	
☐ 25. And the Circus Surprise	8025-7	

☐ 27. Solve A Mystery	8027-3	
☐ 47. At Big Bear Pond	8047-8	
☐ 48. On A Bicycle Trip	8048-6	
☐ 49. Own Little Ferryboat	8049-4	
☐ 50. At Pilgrim Rock	8050-8	
☐ 51. Forest Adventure	8051-6	
☐ 52. At London Tower	8052-4	
☐ 53. In the Mystery Cave	8053-2	
☐ 54. In Volcano Land	8054-0	
☐ 55. And the Goldfish Mystery	8055-9	
☐ 56. And the Big River Mystery	8056-7	
☐ 57. The Greek Hat Mystery	8057-5	
☐ 58. Search for the Green Rooster	8058-3	
☐ 59. And Their Camel Adventure	8059-1	
☐ 60. Mystery of the King's Puppet	8060-5	
☐ 61. And the Secret of Candy Castle	8061-3	
☐ 62. And the Doodlebug Mystery	8062-1	
☐ 63. And the Talking Fox Mystery	8063-X	
☐ 64. The Red, White and Blue Mystery	8064-8	
☐ 65. Dr. Funnybone's Secret	8065-6	
☐ 66. The Tagalong Giraffe	8066-4	
☐ 67. And the Flying Clown	8067-2	
☐ 68. On The Sun-Moon Cruise	8068-0	

SHIP TO:

NAME _____
(please print)

ADDRESS _____

CITY _____ STATE _____ ZIP _____

75-44   Printed in U.S.A.   ☐ 49.

DETACH ALONG DOTTED LINE AND MAIL IN ENVELOPE WITH PAYMENT